THE LADY ONCE KNOWN AS

ABOUT AN EARL
BOOK FIVE

JESS MICHAELS

For Michael, always and forever.

Lily Manning had always loved a wedding, but the one she was currently preparing to attend gave her little pleasure. She watched as her maid held up two gowns for her perusal and flinched.

"I think we decided it was between these two for the ceremony, Mrs. Manning," Susan said. "They're both equally lovely."

Lily tried to maintain her focus on the choice before her and not the emotions boiling in her chest and stomach. "What colors are in Alice's gown, again?" she asked.

"When I spoke to Mary," Susan said, referring to the maid of the bride, "she said there's some pink in the bodice, to offset the ivory and silver."

Lily smiled and at least that wasn't forced. "Pink has always suited my sister. She'll be a beautiful bride. Though she's always lovely."

"It's unfair you haven't been able to see the dress yourself, nor be part of the wedding preparations, if you don't mind my saying so, ma'am," Susan said with a little side glance Lily's way.

Lily shrugged, even though she felt anything but dismissive of *that* topic. "Well, you know how Lady Westinghouse is. Since my father's death, my stepmother has pushed me further and further away from my sister. She always goes on about how I shouldn't be so involved, as Alice and I are only half-blood."

"Hmmph," Susan grunted. "The viscountess didn't say that when she practically let you raise that baby girl. And you just a child yourself."

Lily knew she should correct her servant, gently remind her of her place, but Susan was only saying what she, herself, felt. And it was nice to have someone on her side. Still, it did nothing to reduce the sting of the truth and so she changed the subject.

"The rose gown will complement hers well, then. Let us plan for that one. And if my stepmother makes a fuss over the matching colors, we'll always have the blue to fall back on."

"Very good," Susan said, "I'll pack them both, then, with that in mind. Are you still expecting Lady Delacourt this afternoon?"

"Yes," Lily said, some of her difficult thoughts fading as she thought of her old friend, Esme. Much had changed in her life since they'd been girls together. Since Esme's return to Society after a long, unexplained absence and a sudden marriage to a dashing earl, Lily had felt the shift in her. The increased confidence. Perhaps a little hint that she was a bit more jaded. Still, they'd reconnected happily.

From downstairs, the front bell rang and Lily laughed. "That is probably her now, as if she knew you were talking about her."

"I can finish with the rest, ma'am," Susan said. "And everything will be ready to go for the long journey of the next two days."

"Thank you," Lily called out as she exited the room and headed downstairs. Her butler, Gregson, met her in the hallway. "I've surmised that Lady Delacourt has arrived."

"Indeed, Mrs. Manning, you are correct," Gregson said with a smile. He was a jovial man, though he kept her house in tight order. "She's in the parlor with tea already awaiting you."

"Excellent man, I'll ring if we require anything else." She squeezed his arm and then entered the parlor to find her friend already pouring the tea and arranging biscuits artfully on a plate for them to share.

"Oh, Lily!" Esme said, crossing to kiss each of her cheeks as she entered. "I've already made myself at home."

"I'm glad of it." Lily laughed as Esme returned to the sideboard to fetch a cup and then handed it over. "You've done my job as hostess very well."

"Entirely impolite of me, I know, and I would have waited. My manners haven't slipped so much…or at least I think they haven't. But I admit, I'm *starving*." Esme touched the ever-increasing swell of her stomach beneath her gown. "This baby is going to be as tall as his father from day one, I fear, for all I feed him."

Lily laughed and reached out to gently touch her friend's stomach, a little twinge of pain accompanying the action, despite her joy for Esme. "Well, I could not deny a child whatever they wanted. Or you. Please sit. Tell me *everything* about what is going on in your world."

"The usual," Esme said, settling onto the settee and resting her plate on her stomach with a laugh. "Blissful happiness, punctuated by occasionally being ignored at parties due to my scandalous departure and return to Society."

Lily pursed her lips at the thought. "Well, damn anyone who doesn't accept you with open arms."

Esme gave her hand a squeeze. "Oh, you're kind as always, dearest. But you needn't make that scrunched up face. All I need is the support of my dearest friends, after all, and I'm so lucky in those. I rather like making *them* all whisper behind their fans, especially when Delacourt scandalizes them further with the occasional stolen kiss."

"He doesn't ever hide his ardor, that's certain," Lily said, and once again had to ignore the little twinge of envy.

"And what of *you*? I assume you're all prepared for the trip out to Pembrooke Hills for the wedding next month."

Lily sipped her tea. "Susan and I were just picking my dress for the wedding, itself, and it was the last decision to be made, so all the packing should be finished by now. I'll be off in the morning. I should arrive in two days assuming there are no problems on the road with weather or highwaymen." She shook her head. "Honestly, if a highwayman were to waylay me, I might just run away with him rather than attend this fiasco."

"The lover of a wicked thief, there's an image," Esme said before she tilted her head. "Still have your worries about the marriage then?"

Now Lily had to be careful. "I know Delacourt is friends with the groom."

"He is. Lockhart is a good sort, you know."

"Yes. So you've said," Lily said softly. "But I do know his reputation, after all, don't I? And Alice is so innocent."

"Well, *I* married a rake. Finn's sister Marianne did, as well. And Lockhart's cousin, Clarissa, married one, too. It's a rogues gallery turned fine husbands. I assume Lockhart will be the same."

"Except that you've only named love matches to prove the value of a marriage to one of those from the rogues gallery," Lily mused. "This is not. It's an arrangement and seems to be nothing more, if my sister's letters are to be believed. So while a rake might be tempted to heel by his heart, I do wonder if he would do so for a woman he doesn't love. And if he continues all his wicked behavior without thought for what he has at home, what Alice will feel as a result."

Esme slid a little closer on the settee and touched her hand and suddenly there was sadness in her gaze. Almost pity. "I know your marriage wasn't happy, my dear. It would be impossible for your thoughts not to be painted by that brush."

"I suppose that's true." Lily sighed. "But it's more than the sting of my own past intervening. I so wish to protect Alice. She is very dear to me and since I've been all but removed from her life as of late, I feel this is the best I can do for her. At least once I meet the man, talk to him, I'll have a chance to judge him for his own words and actions, not whatever I believe his character to be. Or, as you put it, through the lens of my own past with Thomas. God or the Devil rest his soul."

Esme snorted out a laugh. "I vote for the Devil, but I'm biased. I do look forward to talking to you about Lockhart again when Finn and I join the party in a week."

"Yes, hopefully I'll be able to greet you with worries washed away and only happiness for my sister remaining." Lily smiled, but she feared that wasn't going to be the case. She feared a great deal, truth be told.

"Enough about that, have you thought about the other thing we discussed the last time we were together?" Esme set her cup and plate aside and arched a fine brow at Lily.

A hot blush was the response Lily couldn't control, for the topic Esme breached was no more comfortable than her worries about Alice's marriage. Perhaps even less so. "Trust you to bring it up so directly."

"I must," Esme said with a little laugh.

"Why?" Lily laughed with her, despite her discomfort. "I *never* should have asked you about it in the first place."

"Asked me about the wonders of physical pleasure after you saw a little too passionate a kiss between my husband and me?" Esme clucked her tongue. "There is *nothing* wrong with that."

"Well, your experience in the marital bed is far different than my own, I fear," Lily said with a sigh as she tried not to think of the awkward groping she had endured and certainly didn't miss.

"Yes, that's too bad." Esme pondered Lily's face then. "I'll repeat what I said to you in that last conversation, you *deserve* the same passion and pleasure and desire as anyone. Before we wed, women of our station are so often told that it can't exist for us. That we shouldn't expect it, but desire is as much the feeling for a woman as it is a man."

"I will likely never know, though. After all, I have no intentions of marrying again."

Esme pressed her lips together. "But you *are* a widow. You have freedom not just financially, but far more with your body. If you took a lover, whether as a longer-term arrangement or something just for a night or two, you couldn't be judged for that."

Lily's cheeks were burning now at the turn of this conversation. It was one thing to talk about the generalities of passion, but to speak of her own? Untenable! "You are being outrageous."

"I'm not even close to being outrageous, you can ask Finn about that," Esme said with a little laugh. "Why do you resist the idea so much? Is it just a lack of experience?"

"Yes." Lily threw up her hands. "Not just in the whole act you're talking about, but in the idea of how one would even find a partner for such a scandalous thing. Does one just enter a club and start shouting for a lover?"

Esme cocked her head. "You're so pretty, that would likely work, yes, but it wouldn't be very subtle. I see your point, though. It isn't easy. Except in places where it is." She worried her lip a little. "Have you...have you ever heard of a hell called the Donville Masquerade?"

Lily blinked. "No. I'm not all that familiar with *any* hells. Is it a gaming establishment?"

"No," Esme said slowly. "There is *some* gaming there, but it's...oh, how do a put this to a lady such as yourself? I am rubbish at this part now." She pondered a moment. "Honesty is the best policy, after all. It's a club for *exactly* the kind of assignations you and I have been discussing."

"For...for sex?" Lily gasped and covered her mouth with her hand as if she could call back the word and the thoughts that followed it.

Esme nodded. "Exactly so. It's well run and managed by a man who does not allow it to be anything but debauched pleasure. Those within its walls are safe, which would be important. But they are also very public, which is my only hesitation. If you went, well, you'd see a great deal more than I think you've ever even imagined.

If you wanted to just watch, you could. If you wanted to choose yourself a lover and burn off some of the tension before you ran off to the wedding, you could do that too."

Lily's mouth dropped open. "Are you talking about *me* going to this place? And going *tonight*?"

Esme shrugged. "If you wish it, I could make all the arrangements. It would be no trouble, for I know the owner and his wife."

"You cannot be serious." Lily's head was beginning to spin with the sudden turn of this conversation. "Whether I have more freedom in my life or not, certainly my going to a place like you've described would end in my shunning."

"Certainly if you weren't careful in places that these, there would be a scandal. But you'd use a false name, you would be masked. No one would know it was you, and even if someone guessed, Marcus Rivers, the proprietor, is very clear about whatever happens in those walls not leaving them. It would be a night without consequences."

Lily blinked. This topic was fraught, but Esme was being entirely seductive about it. And truth be told, it had been changing to watch her friends fall in love and obviously share a passion with their husbands she had never imagined possible for a woman like her. When they talked about it in quiet whispers with dark blushes and bright eyes, she ached a little. *Wanted.*

"Everything has consequences," she whispered. "But that does sound…bewitching. And also like you have a great deal of experience with this place."

There was a moment where Esme's gaze went a little faraway, like she was recalling memories and not all of them pleasant. But then she shook her head. "One day I will tell you where I was and what I did when I was gone from Society. But not today. Would you want me to make the arrangements?"

Lily shifted and worried her hands in her lap. "This is all so fast, it's dizzying."

Esme smiled. "Purposefully so. I want you to answer from your gut, not from some twisted sense of propriety that would keep you from ever doing anything that is just for yourself."

"Yes." Lily said it without even realizing she was going to. Her stomach immediately turned and she swallowed hard, even as Esme caught her hands and bounced a little with excitement.

"Oh, I'm so pleased. You are the dearest person, with such brightness and shine to you. You deserve to have pleasure and secret passions."

Lily's head spun. Pleasure and secret passions. That sounded wild and wonderful and everything opposite of the life she'd led for years and years. The part of her that had been raised with notions of propriety all but beaten into her rebelled against it. Told her she was ruining her prospects with even the thought of such wicked things.

But then reality set in. She was a twenty-eight-year-old widow who had been unable to give her husband children in the seven years they'd been married. Many eligible men would see that as a mark against her if they were looking to marry to create heirs. She had no great fortune to tempt a man in that way, though she had enough to comfortably live the quiet life she'd chosen. There was no future to protect, at least not as tightly as she often did out of... habit, she supposed it was.

But why couldn't she break that habit?

"You look very serious," Esme said, taking her hand and bringing Lily back to the present moment. "Have I pushed too hard?"

"No, I think I needed the push," Lily said with a sigh. "As you said, this should be a night without consequences, yes? And I intend to enjoy it. But oh, I'll need your help. You said the attendees wear masks and I have no idea what kind of gown to choose to potentially seduce a stranger. And how does one do their hair for seduction? Does one rouge their lips or is that too scandalous even for this place?"

Esme laughed and got to her feet. "Come, we'll go up to your chamber and I'll help you with all that. And it will be one more exciting thing to discuss once we all reach the country for the wedding."

Lily smiled as she followed her friend from the parlor, but the mention of the wedding had brought back all her thoughts and worries. And she hoped that tonight, whatever she did or didn't do at the hell, would be a good distraction from the fears she had for her beloved sister.

CHAPTER 2

Viscount George Lockhart rarely wore a mask to the Donville Masquerade. Why bother? He was known as what he was, after all—a rake. *That* was the mask he wore publicly and had all his adult life.

And now it was over. He would ride to his father's country estate tomorrow. A few weeks after that he would be married. It would fulfill an obligation, but...well, the whole thing felt so terribly empty. He sipped his drink and settled into a brood that made the sparkling hell a little less interesting. Or perhaps it was just that he was so jaded that the sex and sin around him didn't mean much. It didn't fire his blood anymore, or at least not the same way.

Sadly, neither did his future bride. He sighed as he thought of her. Miss Westinghouse, and he did only ever think of her as Miss Westinghouse, was beautiful. No one could deny that. She had a friendly face, dark blonde hair and pretty green eyes. If asked, he would have easily described her as striking, for she was undeniably that. And he felt *nothing* about it. There was no zing of desire when he caught a glimpse of her across a room or when she smiled at him. There was certainly no soft, deep sense of connection like he saw between his cousin and her husband or any of his other recently married friends.

George hadn't ever expected such a thing, of course. If someone had asked him a year ago about love he would have scoffed at the idea. It was harder to do so when one was so utterly surrounded by it as he was now. Still, deep feelings hadn't been a criteria when it came to *his* choice in a spouse.

He hadn't *had* criteria really, because he hadn't thought much of it. Until one day a few months ago when his beloved mother had pulled him aside and told him a secret. One that broke his heart. One that drove him to do what she wanted most for him: marry. She'd already created a list of potential brides, he'd picked one with little thought when his emotions were so strong. The contracts had been signed within days and here he was now. About to make the biggest promise of his life.

"Fuck," he grunted, and slugged back the rest of his drink.

"You look like you could use another, friend."

He glanced up at the voice that had interrupted his brood and found Marcus Rivers approaching with a drink in hand. The proprietor of the hell was quite possibly the most interesting person George had ever met. Though he'd been raised under much different circumstances than most of his patrons, he slipped into their ranks with no difficulty. Men wanted to be like him and why not? He had swagger and confidence and an edge that could cut like a knife. He held sway over this den of inequity without raising much more than an eyebrow most nights. And he, like every other person George knew, it seemed, was desperately in love with his wife. Annabelle even helped him run the hell.

"Rivers," he said as the other man sat at the table beside him, and together they looked over the writhing crowd of passionate atten- dees. Couples kissing, touching, playing games that had more to do with sex than chance. There was laughter on the air and desire along with it.

"You don't appear very happy for a man who is about to take a bride," Rivers said after a moment.

George snorted. "I'd say you were a mind reader, but I don't think I've kept my expression schooled well tonight."

"If it's not something you desire, then I'm sorry about it, Lockhart," Rivers said. "Truly. Your world doesn't always allow for deeper feeling or passion, I know."

"You'll be extra sorry soon, I think, for I know I'm one of your best patrons and I won't be attending the masquerade much anymore. If at all."

"No?" Rivers asked, his eyebrows lifting in what seemed like surprise at the statement.

George shook his head. "It wouldn't be fair to her, would it?"

Rivers gave a slight smile. "Ah, I knew you were a good man under all that rakish charm. So you intend to be a faithful husband, do you?"

"I would like to be better than I was raised to be, I think," George said softly, thinking of his father's mistresses over the years and how the existence of them had hurt his mother. The earl had slowed down in his later years and his parents had seemed to have come to an accord as of late, but it didn't erase the betrayals. The hurts. The humiliations. Their bond, whatever it had been at the beginning, had been damaged. George's mother hadn't even yet told his father that same awful secret she'd shared with him.

"Then this is your last night? Your last hurrah, it seems," Rivers said, which thankfully jolted George from his thoughts.

"Indeed." George drank the second drink as quickly as he had the first. Already he felt the little tingle of his senses dulling. Just enough to take the edge off.

"Then I suggest you go enjoy it rather than sitting at my table looking like a man about to be led to the gallows," Rivers said. "There is pleasure aplenty to drown your sorrows in."

He got up and George joined him. Rivers clapped him on the arm and said goodnight before he slipped off into the crowd.

George let out a great sigh and looked around, this time with more purpose. Rivers was right. He could brood anywhere. The reason he'd come here tonight was to drive out his troubles in the warm body of some willing lady. He had to go on the hunt, for the last time, perhaps.

He drew a breath and looked around the room. There were women galore to choose from. Unlike him, most of them were masked, but he knew there were all kinds here, from the highest duchess to the cyprians using the safety of this place to establish their relationships and settle themselves. Some he recognized as women he had indulged with before, but none drew his eye, even if he'd enjoyed his time with them. It was intensely frustrating, to be here for his final meal before the execution and find himself not hungry.

At least until *she* walked through the crowd. A woman in a deeply cut red gown and plain black mask, dark hair bound up loosely, soft curls bobbing around her cheeks and shoulders in a tempting waterfall that made a man want to trace the same path with his lips. He leaned forward, almost not of his own volition, tracking her graceful movements. Did he know her? It felt like there was some connection there, something instantaneous and hot that made him think he might have bedded her before. But no. He searched his memory and couldn't find her there in the tangled, foggy collection of merging bodies and mouths.

It was just that she drew him to her. Like a siren. He stepped a little closer, ignoring anything and everything else in the room but her. *She* was not as focused. Her dark eyes drifted from one place to another and beneath the edge of her mask, he could see her cheeks were pink with high color. Arousal or shock? Perhaps both. There was a tremble to those full lips that gave him the impression. Perhaps it was her first night here, perhaps she'd never seen such shocking things as the debauched pleasures going on around her.

He knew only one thing: he was going to find out. And if she was an innocent to the Donville Masquerade, he was very happy to be her introduction to all it had to offer.

He moved toward her, drawing a hand over his clothing to smooth it. One step, another, and he noted the moment she became aware of his approach. Her eyes met his. Stunning eyes. Brown, but they sparkled in the candle and lamplight of the hell, filled with life and emotion. Her lips parted as that same gaze drifted over him from head to toe and made his body react along the same line as her stare.

He hadn't had such a strong response to a woman in a very long time. He'd almost forgotten how intoxicating that could be.

"Good evening," he said as he reached her.

That pretty gaze flitted away toward the door and escape for a moment before she pushed her shoulders back and swallowed hard. "Good evening," she said, but her voice barely carried and was rough.

He smiled in the hopes it would soothe her. "It's a little over-whelming your first time, I know."

She blinked and there was no mistaking her surprise at the statement. "How—how do you know it's my first time here?"

He leaned a little closer. "You have the look about you. A little like a rabbit trying to avoid a trap."

"And would that make you the hunter, sir?"

He shrugged. "Anyone can be a hunter in the Donville Masquer-ade..." He hesitated in the hopes she would provide a name. It wouldn't be her real one, but it would give him something to moan into her ear if this night ended as he hoped it would.

She worried her lip, forcing him to look at the fullness again. Wonder what it would taste like if he nipped it gently as she rose beneath him in pleasure. "I can't—it's—"

He cocked his head. "Not your real name."

"Oh. Yes." She let out a shaky sigh. "I suppose I *do* reveal myself as naive, don't I? My name...or at least my name here...is Aphrodite."

His brows lifted. "*Aphrodite?*"

Her cheeks brightened further. "Very silly, isn't it? I didn't pick it."

He drew back at that statement. He'd thought this woman was a lady based on her hesitation, but now he wondered if she was a lightskirt. And perhaps not one here of her own volition if she hadn't even chosen her own secret name.

"If you're in trouble," he said softly. "You have those here who would help. I can bring you to Rivers. He and his wife would never let you be harmed."

She shook her head. "I-I don't know what you mean."

"You said you didn't choose your name, I thought you might have been forced to come here," he explained.

"That is a surprisingly protective reflex, sir," she said after a brief hesitation, and her tone was now speculative, as if she had seen something in him she hadn't expected. "Do you often play the hero to distressed damsels?"

"I do my best not to play the villain."

She nodded slowly. "Let me put your mind at ease. I *wasn't* forced in any way to come here. At least not by someone monstrous who wielded power over me. A dear friend encouraged me to attend, one who is far more experienced in the ways of the world than I. *She* chose my name, much to my chagrin once she told me what to use at the door and throughout the night."

She smiled and he caught his breath. He could hardly focus on anything but the brilliance of it as he nodded. "Good. I'm-I'm glad to hear it."

"And what about *you?*" she asked. "You're clearly a much more experienced member of the club, but how did you find yourself here the first time you attended?"

He blinked. "I can…hardly recall," he admitted. "I don't think any lady has ever asked me that."

"I'm happy to be unique in the question, as long as it doesn't offend," she said.

"It would take a great deal more than a question to offend me." He tilted his head. "Why don't you guess at it, though?"

"Guess at how you came to be a member here?" She looked around with a shiver, as if she'd just recalled the forbidden pleasures going on around them. Her gaze darted for a moment, pupils dilating. His body clenched at the sight of her desire, hesitant but there. His for the plucking. But not yet. The game was too pleasurable at present.

He nodded in answer to her question. "I've always wondered what Aphrodite would think of me."

She laughed, the sound a little low and husky. "The true Aphrodite would likely not even bat an eye at everything around her. She'd be so bored and jaded by it all."

Bored and jaded. He'd just been labeling himself the same way. He certainly didn't feel it now. Not when she licked her lips and looked him up and down before she spoke again.

"It's different for men, isn't it? All of this."

He had asked a playful question, but her answer didn't feel playful now. It was almost mesmerizing, like she was peeling the layers of both of them away and leaving something real at the core. Something no one else saw.

"I suppose it is," he said softly.

"I imagine you came here years ago, perhaps even while you were in school. Brought by some older friend or cousin who was older. Wiser. More experienced. Someone who thought you would enjoy how shocking it all was. Were you shocked the first time? Did it all frighten and thrill you, as it does me?"

He stared at her a moment, this woman who at this moment only had a goddess's name but felt more real than anyone else he'd spent time with lately while he was in the fog of pain and worry. She made him recall parts of himself he hadn't visited in a long time. "I was eighteen," he said. "My birthday, actually. And yes, it was an older cousin who paid for my membership that first time. I wasn't entirely inexperienced, but I was certainly shocked by what I saw here. By what I felt when I watched it all."

"Like you're hungry and trembly and hot all over," she whispered.

He nodded. "Yes. That. Over time I think I forgot it. Perhaps I forgot a great deal." He wrinkled his brow. "This has become a very serious conversation."

She smiled a little and the spell was broken. "You'll regret approaching me if I drag you into such maudlin thoughts."

"Never. Though I admit it's very odd to have a lovely masked stranger make such an accurate measure of me. Perhaps as recompense you might dance with me."

She looked over her shoulder toward the dancefloor where couples were paired off, grinding together in ways that never would have been accepted in any ballroom in Society. Mouths merged, hands roved, it was all foreplay. In some cases, more than foreplay. There was shock to her expression, but there was much more beyond it. So much more.

"Yes," she whispered, this time with a little more neediness to her tone. It called to him, beckoned to his own desire.

He held out a hand and she looked at it. It was ungloved, of course. The Donville Masquerade was a place for skin on skin. She looked at her own ungloved fingers for a moment and then took his hand. There was a shock of electricity that rippled up his arm when she did, a fascinating power that made his body tingle. At least he knew this last night before the wedding would be explosive.

They moved to the dancefloor together and she shivered before she lifted her hand to his shoulder. He held her stare as they began to move, his hand dipping low on her hip, tracing the line of her there as his thumb stroked against silk.

She gasped at the contact and stumbled slightly, but he kept her upright as they turned in the milling crowd.

"What—what is your name?" she asked. "Or the name you give here."

So she didn't recognize him. That gave him even more clues to who she was. She wasn't a lady of his rank, then, or at least not one who moved regularly in his circles. He started at that thought, for he'd never been so interested in the origins of a lover at the masquerade before. Why was this woman different?

"If you are Aphrodite," he said softly, "then let me be Ares."

She stared up at him. "Her lover?"

His nod was slow and meant to give his exact meaning. "*If* she would allow it."

Her breath hitched and he could see the hesitance again. A little fear, or at least nervousness, at the idea. "This is what *she* came for," she said at last. "But she…*I*…the reality is different than the fantasy."

"Hopefully better," he said. "May we try something to see?"

Her eyes went wide, impossibly wide. "What is that?"

He didn't answer with words, but slowly dipped his head to kiss her. She didn't pull away from the slow descent. In fact, she lifted on her tiptoes with a shivering sigh. When their mouths met, her lips were soft, as full against his as they looked when she spoke.

And, oh, how he wanted her. More now that he had this tiny taste. He traced her lips with his tongue, she opened immediately and her hand tightened against his shoulder. He drew her up closer, tight against his body and delved into the kiss further, exploring her mouth with thorough intent. Thoughts of his future faded, leaving only her and this and what he wanted to do next.

Oh, yes. His last night was going to be explosive, indeed.

∽

Lily had been kissed before. Or, at least, she thought she had. Kissing hadn't been something that happened all that often with Thomas, but it had occasionally been something they shared. But this kiss with this man in this scandalous place was nothing like anything she'd ever felt before. It was a possession, a claiming, as he explored her mouth with his heated, talented tongue that tasted a little of fine whisky and whispered promises. He held her like possession, too, one hand gripping her hip, the other cradling her back like he'd keep her upright if her trembling knees at last gave out. It was a distinct possibility and she couldn't help but feel protected by the action.

At last their mouths parted and for a moment they only stared at each other. He looked as stunned as she felt, though that wasn't possible. This was clearly a man who was well-versed in seduction. Someone who belonged in this hell of sin and pleasure, even if he'd admitted to his nervousness years and years ago.

He was also quite possibly the most beautiful man she'd ever seen in her life. She was still startled by that as she stared up at him. He was tall and lean with dark hair that was just a little too long and rakishly messy. He had a scruff of facial hair that only seemed to accentuate the lines of his hard jaw and the fullness of the lips that had just claimed hers. And his blue-gray eyes were impossible to escape as they pinned her in her place, watching every movement of her face.

"Come in the back with me," he said, his voice rough.

The request...or was it an order? Whatever it was, it moved through her with as much heat as his touch. It was equally terrifying, as well. With everything going on in the open around them, she could only imagine how much further things would go in the back.

She swallowed, trying to find words. He tilted his head. "*This* is what you came for, isn't it, Aphrodite, goddess of love and passion and pleasure?"

She shivered and then she slowly nodded because she couldn't find the words. He leaned down again and his lips brushed hers a second time. "Then let me give it to you. Everything you've ever fantasized about, let me give it to you."

"Yes."

She said it without meaning to, just as she had when he asked her to dance, because this man was irresistible. What he offered was powerful and terrifying all at once. But she'd come here for a night without consequences and he seemed just the man to give it.

He took her hand and lifted it to his lips, his breath warm on her knuckles before he kissed them. When he guided her forward, she followed, letting him lead her through the writhing crowd that had so fascinated her when she first entered the hell and now seemed to fade so that there was only him in focus. They reached the back of the big room and he signaled to a man on guard before a dimly lit hallway. She followed him farther down that hallway to a room.

When he opened the door and motioned for her to go in, she caught her breath. Somehow she'd pictured the chamber would be stark, but it was anything but. It was sumptuous, richly appointed with fine wallpaper, dark furniture and a bed covered in silk sheets. A fire glowed on the opposite side of the room, warming the air and making everything seem soft.

Except him. As he shut the door and leaned against it, watching her take everything in, he was anything but soft. When she faced him, he extended a finger and crooked it to bring her back to him. There was almost no choice but to do as the motion required. She moved to him and gasped when he caught her hand and brought her up against him again. He kissed her, deeper now, more slowly and she whimpered against his lips.

"If you want me to stop, just say the word," he said softly.

She drew back and stared up into those remarkable eyes. He was offering escape. She could take it and run away and forget this had ever happened. Perhaps that would have been better. Certainly it would have been more proper. And yet she couldn't. More to the point, she didn't want to.

So she took a shaky breath and whispered, "Don't stop."

CHAPTER 3

Never in her life had Lily been so bold as she was now. When she'd attempted anything even approaching a surrender of propriety in what she said or wore or did, it had almost always led to consequences. It didn't appear there would be any of those tonight. When she told this man not to stop, a wicked smile quirked his lips and he backed her toward the bed. When they reached it, he pivoted her so her back faced him and began to unfasten the buttons on her scandalously low-cut dress. Esme had insisted she borrow it tonight after they disregarded all her regular gowns. Every moment, she'd felt wicked in it. Now she felt even more wicked as he pushed it forward and leaned in to kiss the skin he exposed along her spine.

"You've done this before?" he asked, breathless.

She turned to look at him. "Yes. I-I was married. He's gone now."

His gaze moved over her face. She wasn't certain what he was searching for, perhaps whatever emotion she felt about that fact. Perhaps something else. He was too hard to read. She hoped she was, too, because she didn't want the past or the future to interrupt this night. Not now when she was so close to something she ached for in a way she never had before.

"How long has it been?" he asked.

"He's been dead almost two years," she said. "And he...he never looked at me the way you're looking at me. Like you'll devour me whole."

Once again the corners of his lips twitched for a wicked little smile. "Devour you whole. There's an idea."

He slipped a finger beneath the drooping neckline of her gown and slowly tugged so that the satin fell away, down her arms and revealed her from the waist up.

Esme had told her that she couldn't wear underthings with a dress like this and so Lily was naked beneath. He stared at her exposed body, his pupils dilating and licked his lips. She was put to mind of their earlier conversation about the bunny and the hunter.

She'd never felt more like a helpless little bunny in her life. Or more exposed. She wanted to lift her hands to cover herself, but fought the desire. He already thought her naïve, she didn't want to make that worse. What if he bored of it and walked away? Now that she was here, she didn't want that. She wanted whatever he would do. She wanted it so much that her legs clenched, her hands trembled, the low ache between her thighs felt like fire in her bloodstream.

"You are stunning," he whispered. "My God."

Whatever heat that had rushed to her cheeks when her body was revealed increased now with the soft sincerity of that compliment. She was humiliated that her eyes filled with tears at it, that she yearned for that praise as much as she longed for his heated touch.

His expression softened even as she blinked to try to keep the tears at bay. He said nothing about them, only moved closer and pushed the gown down her hips as he kissed her once more.

She wound her arms up around his neck, rising up to his mouth with a gasp as her breasts rubbed against the front of his jacket. His hands dipped down, cupping her backside, squeezing it as he ground against her and she felt the evidence of his desire hard against her stomach.

When they broke apart this time, his gaze was more wild, his breath shorter. He pointed to the bed. "Lie down."

She nodded and lay back on the impossibly soft bedclothes. He stared at her a moment, then blinked and backed away to begin unfastening his cravat. He shed his clothing swiftly, efficiently, and it was clear that this was something he did a great deal. He never stopped looking at her even as he tugged his shirt over his head.

And she couldn't have stopped looking at him even if she were offered all the gold in England. She sat up, staring at the expanse of lean muscle of his chest and stomach, peppered with chest hair that led in a fascinating trail down into the waist of his trousers. The trousers he was unbuttoning and pushing aside with the rest.

"Oh," she whispered as his cock bounced free, hard and ready and impressive. Not that she had a lot to compare it to, but he definitely won the battle.

"Your eyes are very wide," he whispered as he pressed his hands on the bottom of the bed and began to make his way to her. "I cannot wait to see what they do when I make you come."

He touched her bare calves, his lean fingers gliding there. She arched as heat sizzled in the wake of his hands. Had she ever felt such a way? Or had Thomas even ever touched her like that, had his hands ever trailed up her knees and made her shake? She didn't recall. She hardly recalled her own name as this man's fingers pressed into her thighs, pushed to make her widen her legs.

She did and watched as he looked at her. He licked his lips and she expected him to press inside of her immediately. But he didn't. Instead he trailed his hands up her hips and finally cupped her breasts in each palm, stoking gently, rhythmically and setting her on fire.

His head lowered, not to her lips but to one hard nipple, and he swirled his tongue in a languid circle around and around. She arched with a cry, her hands coming down into those thick locks of hair and he chuckled against her skin.

"And here we've barely begun," he murmured, his gaze coming up to hers even though he didn't lift his head.

She twisted beneath him as he shifted to her opposite breast, lavishing her with the same attention there as he had before. By the time he began to trail his hot mouth down to her stomach with his lips, she was shaking. She'd never before felt something like this, this fire in her blood that made her so aware of every part of her body. Most especially the parts he licked and nipped as he brushed his bearded cheek against her hip, her thigh, and finally he pressed his hand between her legs.

She should have felt embarrassed to be so intimately caressed by a stranger. She should have been trying to escape his gaze on her most private of parts. Instead she lifted toward him, wantonly giving over what he so brazenly claimed and wishing she knew how to ask for whatever would come next.

He didn't make her wait long. He massaged the outer lips of her sex with his fingers, then he parted her and she felt the brush of his tongue between her legs. She jolted against the electric sensation, rising to meet him in this new, wonderful explosion of heat and pleasure.

He made a low growl from deep his chest, an animal, claiming sound. One hand settled more firmly on her hip, holding her in place as he began to lick her in earnest. She rocked against him, the sensation building rapidly now, unlike anything she'd ever known or felt, not with her husband, not with her own furtive hand in the dark.

This was something far more magical and the waves of it built powerfully and swiftly until at last she felt the edge of the pleasure right there. He sucked her clitoris and she fell, gasping and crying out as wave after unstoppable wave wracked her.

He moaned against her skin, vibrations from the sound only increasing the pleasure that seemed to ricochet out of control through every part of her body. If the man had told her she glowed, if she had levitated off the bed, she wouldn't have been surprised.

At last, the sensations eased a fraction, their sharp edges smoothing even as little earthquakes continued through her body. Only then did he lift his head, rise up over her once again and claim her mouth with the same fervor with which he had claimed her sex. She tasted her own pleasure on his lips and gasped at that erotic knowledge, digging her nails into his shoulders as he wedged his hips between hers.

She felt the head of him at her entrance, braced for pain or discomfort as he took her, but he slid home in her body without any resistance. Just one smooth thrust and there was only pleasure. There was only heat. There was only him and them and this.

She lifted beneath him as he moaned again into her neck as if she moved him as much as he moved her. How could that be possible? She forgot the question as he drove hard into her body, taking with sure, steady strokes. She met him without hesitation, driving him to release, driving herself back to the same edge. And when she found it again she couldn't stop herself from gripping her legs around his hips, from moaning and crying out without a care for who could hear the echo in the hallway.

He joined her with a roar and then withdrew, spending into his hand and across her stomach in thick ropes of release. He collapsed down over her, pressing kisses to her neck, her collarbone and finally her lips. The kiss gentled at last and they broke apart.

She was shaking with all that had happened. With the pleasure, yes, but also the knowledge that she had surrendered herself so fully to man whose real name she didn't even know. And now that same man rolled to his side and cradled her against his broad chest, smoothing a hand against her neck with such gentleness that she almost believed she could stay this way forever.

She had to recall she couldn't. Except as she snuggled into his arms, reveling in the feeling of being held as much as she had in being taken, she pushed away that thought. She could extract herself later. For now, she would just enjoy this moment.

~

In all the times George had come to the Donville Masquerade and bedded a lover, he'd never lain in that lover's arms afterward. This wasn't the place for romantic notions, for sweetness. He took, he thanked, he left.

Only as he held this woman in his arms, he felt no drive to flee the chamber. He only wanted to revel in the aftermath of what might have been the most powerful encounter he'd ever experienced.

"I never knew it could be like that," she said softly.

He looked down at her. Her mask still covered half her face, hiding her identity, but it couldn't hide the wonder and the sadness of those bright eyes. He felt an instant desire to ease the second, to encourage the first. As a rake who had lazily fucked his way through life until now, neither was a comfortable desire. And yet he couldn't resist somehow.

"It wasn't with your husband?" he asked while he gently untangled a chestnut curl from the tie of her mask.

Her lips thinned and the sadness in her increased. "We had an arranged marriage. I was very young, he was…well, he wasn't. I'm sorry, I shouldn't trouble you with all this."

"I asked. I want to know, if you want to share."

She let out a shaky sigh and then continued, "I-I tried to love him. I tried to want him, but it didn't work. There was nothing there and in the end, it was all very empty."

"I'm sorry," George said, and meant it. For both of them. After all, wasn't he about to enter the exact same scenario? Miss Westinghouse inspired no desire nor deeper feelings in him. She was twelve years younger than he, just eighteen. When they talked it was always of surface things because they had nothing else in common, or at least nothing he'd found yet.

Would they end up just the way this siren in his arms had with her late husband? Empty? When he was dead, would she feel nothing about it but relief?

"Is that why you came here tonight?" he asked, shoving those desperate thoughts aside so they didn't mar this perfect experience. "To experience what you never did with him?"

She shrugged. "I didn't give much thought to it at the time, honestly. Many marriages are like that, aren't they? At least I was told it's a way of our world. But then recently my friends began to marry and they were all in *love*. So much love, so much passion, you couldn't avoid seeing it, feeling it pulse in the air. It was like being put in a prison of other people's desire. What I believed was normal and to be expected suddenly became sad and pathetic. My life shrank. And, yes, I wanted to feel a little bit of what I now realize I missed. So I came here."

He stared down at her. She was telling a story so like his own that it surprised him to hear it from another person's lips. "And I did I fulfill that?"

"Oh, yes," she whispered, and reached up to trace his lips gently. Her fingers were so soft against his mouth, so comforting. He could have lain like that forever, died in her arms and been perfectly content with this one, shattering night.

He blinked. But he couldn't, could he? This was his last stand and he had taken it. Tomorrow he would leave London and go to be a groom to some other woman. And so he had to extract himself from this shocking connection that only seemed to grow with each word spoken. To do anything else was unfair to all parties.

"I'm glad of it," he said, shifting reluctantly.

She rolled away from his arms and watched him as he got up and tugged on his trousers. There was a hint of disappointment on her face. She wanted him to stay as much as he wished to. That somehow made it all worse that they both felt that unexpected connection, that powerful longing, that could now not be explored or fulfilled.

"I hope I satisfied you, as well…Ares," she said. "Even though I wasn't experienced or likely very talented in such things."

He froze in his gathering of his things and pivoted back to her. "We're strangers," he said softly. "Who will likely never meet again, so I'll be honest with you even if I should not. Tonight was remarkable. *You* are remarkable. And I won't forget this, no matter what comes next." He leaned down and kissed her once more.

Her arms came around his neck and she expelled a broken sigh against his lips. Everything in him told him to collapse back into the bed with her. Or to gather her up and run away with her, figure out the rest later.

He didn't. He pulled away instead and bent to pick up her discarded gown. "Now then, let me help you dress."

She nodded and got up, but as he assisted her and finished dressing himself, as they walked out of the back room together, their fingers intertwined before they reached the outer hall with all its debauchery and sound and light, he couldn't help but feel he lost something.

And that left an ache in his chest that he hadn't expected when he kissed her knuckles at last and they parted with only one final glance of farewell.

CHAPTER 4

Thanks to a sudden, heavy rainstorm, the journey to Pembrooke Hills took half a day longer than it should have. Normally that would have troubled Lily, for she hated to be late. Even on time felt a little like too far for her taste.

But this time? This time she had welcomed the extra hours to herself in the journey because she couldn't stop thinking of her night at the Donville Masquerade with the mysterious man, her Ares. She shivered even now as she flashed to the feeling of the brush of his soft beard on her thighs, his mouth on her sex, his eyes boring into hers and giving her a glimpse of...

Well, it was best not to ponder what she'd had a glimpse of in those startling gray-blue eyes. It felt too strong and instant and foolish to believe it could have truly been there. Was she so pathetic that she felt a powerful deeper connection with a stranger where there was only surface pleasure?

"Are you well, Mrs. Manning?"

She blinked and looked across the seat toward Susan. Her maid had given up engaging her much in conversation in the last day because of Lily's increasing distraction. But now Susan frowned as she looked at her.

"Oh, I'm fine, just enjoying the scenery," Lily lied, and motioned out the window to the bright green of the rolling hills as they neared Pembrooke Hills and the estate and wedding gathering waiting there for them.

"You seem…troubled," Susan pressed. "Are you still worried about Miss Alice?"

Lily cleared her throat. She ought to thank Susan because *this* was what she needed to focus on, not a night that would never be repeated. And if her face was so readable that her troubles were clear to her maid, she definitely had to refocus because she didn't want to reveal that vulnerability to strangers, nor to her stepmother, who had often taken any opportunity to strike against Lily in the past.

"I suppose I can't help but worry," she admitted. "I know so little about the man my sister is to marry. And what I do know cannot do anything but trouble me."

"Especially after your own marriage, if you don't mind my saying," Susan said with a frown.

It was a cheeky observation, perhaps one that a servant shouldn't have made, but Susan was one of the few who knew how bleak Lily's marriage had been. She hadn't shared the deepest truths with many people.

The stranger who had taken her to bed had somehow become one of them. She should have regretted that, but it was too easy to tell him her secrets when he was holding her like she was his. Like he would protect her, soothe her, give her—

No. She had to stop doing that. It was over, *done*, and she had to move forward. And this was the perfect time, for the carriage was pulling through a fine iron gate and down a twisting, well-tended lane. Both she and Susan leaned closer to the window and sucked in twin gasps as the fine manor came into view. It was a stunning in its white stone glory, with an enormous portico and sparkling leaded windows glinting in the sunshine.

"And one day she will be countess over all this," Lily mused.

Susan shook her head. "Hard to imagine, for I always picture her as a little girl."

Lily nodded. She did the same. But her sister, though just eighteen, would grow into this role over time. It would be made easier if her husband helped her in that. Gave her space and assistance in learning to be viscountess and later take the roll of countess when his father died and he inherited that higher title.

Would a rake known for his lovers and playful lack of care be willing to do that for a woman he didn't love? Those questions continued to batter her.

The carriage pulled to a stop and Lily reached across to squeeze Susan's hand. "I'm sorry I wasn't a better travel companion, dearest Susan."

Her maid smiled at her gently. "You've never been anything but kind your whole life, Mrs. Manning, you're always a fine companion. Now I'll get your chamber all arranged while you take care of the meeting and greeting of the family and this man who shall take our Miss Alice to such heights."

"Thank you," Lily said, and took the hand of the servant that extended into the carriage to assist her onto the drive. She greeted him and said a few words to her footman and driver before she headed up the stairs to the butler waiting on the portico.

"Mrs. Manning," he intoned. "I'm Reeves, the family butler. We're so pleased to have you join us."

"Good afternoon, Reeves," she said. "My apologies for the delay in my arrival. I hope it didn't put your staff out."

"Not at all." He followed her into the foyer of the grand house and took her hat and gloves. "The family is gathered in the parlor for their tea and has been advised of your arrival. You may join them if you don't immediately wish to be taken to your room."

The sharp edge of nervousness rose in her chest, but she pushed it aside. "It will take my maid a little while to get my arrangements ready, so I'll happily join the family." He inclined his head and then led her down a long, twisting hallway, past dozens of rooms. "It's a beautiful home."

The butler gave her a small smile over his shoulders. "Indeed, madam, we are proud of it. The family has lived in Pembrooke Hills for over two hundred years, since they replaced the older castle with this more modern home."

"A castle," she said, eyes widening. It wasn't entirely uncommon for the odd family castle to exist, but she'd never known a person who actually owned one. That made it sound like her sister would be a princess.

"Yes. Most of it is gone, but there is an old tower that remains on the old site. I'm sure Lord Lockhart would be happy to take you on a tour. He used to love it as a boy."

They reached a closed door and behind it Lily could hear the faint murmur of voices and light laughter. Her heart leapt, for in a moment she would see her beloved sister who she hadn't been able to see for months. And she would meet the man who would marry Alice and hopefully protect her. Or at least not hurt her.

Reeves opened the door and intoned, "Mrs. Manning, my lord, my ladies."

As Lily stepped into the room, she instantly found her sister first and watched Alice jump to her feet. She raced toward Lily, her sweet face lit up with the same joy Lily felt in her own heart. Just before she was enveloped in a hug, she saw her stepmother, Prudence, purse her lips in displeasure.

"Oh, Lily!" Alice burst out, pulling back. "I'm so happy you're here!"

"As am I!" She searched her sister's face. Alice looked more like her mother than Lily, with her blonde curls and dark blue eyes, but when she smiled it was the same expression Lily saw in the mirror sometimes and that made her happy.

Alice grasped her hand and drew her toward the others in the room. Now she focused on them. There were two couples alongside her stepmother and sister. One was older, she assumed Lockhart's parents. The other was closer to her own age, and she recalled that Lockhart's cousin and her husband were also to be in attendance to the family part of the gathering.

"May I present my sister, Mrs. Manning," Alice said. "Lily, this is the Earl and Countess of Pembrooke."

Lily gave a small curtsey. "My lord, my lady, what a pleasure to make your acquaintance at last."

The earl inclined his head politely, though with seemingly little interest. But the countess, a very pretty, petite woman with a round, friendly face, stepped forward. "And we yours. We have heard so much about you from your dear sister, I feel as though I know you."

"And this is the Earl and Countess of Kirkwood," Alice continued, motioning to the other couple. "Lockhart's dearest cousin and her husband. They were recently married, just a few months ago."

Lady Kirkwood stepped forward and took Lily's hand in her own. "Mrs. Manning, it's such a pleasure. I believe we share another mutual friend beyond your delightful sister."

"We do," Lily said with a wide smile of her own at the acknowledgment. "I have heard wonderful things about you from Esme—Lady Delacourt. And I'm so happy to make your acquaintance."

She was happy to see Lady Kirkwood's expression light up with as much joy at the mention of Esme as Lily herself felt. Esme deserved good friends who stood by her. She might have continued the conversation with the lady, but Alice squeezed her arm.

"Let me fetch your tea," her sister insisted, and rushed to the sideboard.

"Good afternoon, Prudence," Lily said, glancing toward her step-mother at last.

The viscountess sniffed lightly. "Lily. You are late."

Heat suffused Lily's cheeks and she immediately felt guilty even though she'd done nothing to cause her own tardiness. "Oh yes, I know. The weather just outside London slowed our progress the first day. I do apologize for the inconvenience it might have caused."

"None at all," Lady Pembrooke said, motioning to a chair that had been unoccupied. "Though I am sorry that you were not also greeted by Lockhart. He is a little late himself from a ride around the estate, but should be back soon."

Lily pursed her lips briefly but forced a smile as Alice came to her with a cup of tea. Her sister then took the chair beside hers and grasped one hand just as she always had when she was a little girl.

So her fiancé couldn't even bother to join his future wife for tea. One more little mark against him, for his tardiness couldn't be explained away so easily as her own, certainly. It could be for lack of care. Or pure selfishness. Neither would be good answers to all the questions that boiled within her.

She pushed the thoughts away. "It is no trouble. There was no way to anticipate my arrival and I'm certain I will have plenty of time in the next few weeks before the wedding to make his acquaintance."

She glanced at Alice and noted the slight tightness of her lips, but then the small group launched into conversation and she fell into the politeness of getting to know them all.

It was impossible not to like Lord and Lady Kirkwood. They were both friendly and the countess was very kind, especially to Alice. Lily had believed they would be friends after everything Esme had shared about the woman, but she knew it now.

The Earl and Countess of Pembrooke were also easy with her sister, though the gentleman was not particularly engaged and she thought she sensed a slight tension to the countess. That hesitation that didn't seem to have to do with Alice, thank heavens, but something else.

She was beginning to find some ease and comfort when the door to the parlor opened and the group began to rise for the newcomer.

"Forgive my lateness," said the male voice behind her. "Carson and Ward were doing some work in the old castle site and one of the horses thew a shoe, so I assisted in fixing that."

Lily caught her breath. That voice felt so familiar. Slowly she turned and it felt like every light in the world went out except for a piercing spotlight on the man standing in the doorway, still speaking although she had no idea what was being said anymore.

It was *him*. The man from the Donville Masquerade.

Oh, he had neatly trimmed his hair and shaved his beard so that the rakishly effortless mess of him was hidden. He was dressed more formally. But it was definitely him.

"Lily." It was Alice's voice saying her name and Lily fought to surface from her shock. "Come and meet Lockhart."

Lily's stomach turned and the tea she had drank lifted all the way to her throat and threatened to cast itself back up. No. No, that couldn't be correct. The man standing there, the man who had pleasured her not three nights before, was *Lockhart*? Her sister's future husband? A man Lily had so many questions and fears about?

This was the fantasy man who had made her feel things that still haunted her every dream, and she feared would continue to do so until she took her last breath?

Her world felt like it was collapsing and she barely stayed on her feet as she stepped forward and extended a trembling hand.

~

George stared at the woman coming across the parlor toward him, her hand outstretched, but also slightly shaking as she stared at him with unblinking eyes. He'd never met Mrs. Manning, his intended's older sister, though Miss Westinghouse had mentioned her a few times in conversations he had frankly forgotten along with much else they discussed.

He took the woman's hand and for a moment there was a flutter of electricity that surged between them. She was truly beautiful now that he really looked at her. She had dark hair, bright brown eyes and full lips. But it was her expression that continued to draw him in. She looked something between terrified and sick as she choked out, "Lord Lockhart, a-a pleasure to make your acquaintance at last."

She withdrew her hand immediately and stepped back, her gaze dropping away, darting toward her sister instead.

"And yours, Mrs. Manning," he said with a smile he hoped would soothe whatever was troubling her.

Instead she pivoted away from him and returned to her seat, refusing to meet his stare.

Did he know this woman? As the others continued talking, he moved his gaze to her. It felt like he might. Was that why she was having such a strong reaction to him? Had he slighted her? Or worse, flirted with her at some boring party he didn't even recall?

He moved to the sideboard and prepared himself tea. When he turned back to the group with cup in hand, he found Mrs. Manning watching him, but she jerked her gaze down again when he met it. Flummoxed, he took a seat beside his parents on the settee and tried to focus in on the conversation with his family and that of his intended.

It was mostly light chatter about nothing at all. He noted that Mrs. Manning didn't engage in most of it, even as her sister and his cousin Clarissa continued to make efforts to draw her out. She always responded when they did, but there was no point when she looked at George again.

Eventually they all finished their tea and rose. Lady Westing-house began a conversation with Kirkwood and Clarissa. This left Miss Westinghouse to draw Mrs. Manning to the window across the room and motion to the beautiful expanse of the garden that was in view, as well as the rolling hills beyond. Unlike when his intended spoke to him, Miss Westinghouse was animated with her sister. And Mrs. Manning was certainly more at ease with her sister, smiling, though the expression was tight and remained troubled.

"You said there was some trouble at the old castle site."

George jumped as he realized his parents had joined him at the sideboard while he watched the two women talk. "Er, yes. It's all fine now."

"Good." His father shook his head. "I'll speak to Carson and Ward later and verify it."

George forgot his confusion about Mrs. Manning's reaction to him and pursed his lips. That was his father. Despite the fact that George was near thirty and a viscount in his own right, the earl still sometimes treated him like he was ten. "If you feel you must," he said softly.

His mother slid her hand through his elbow and gently squeezed. He glanced down at her, softening his expression.

"If you'll all excuse me," the earl said to the room at large, bent his head toward his wife and then slipped from the room.

George sighed. "I suppose he'll believe Carson and Ward at least."

His mother shrugged. "I doubt he'll believe anyone until he looks at the shoes of the horses, then inspects the site himself. You know how he is."

"Heavy handed?" George said. "Indeed, I do."

His mother's frown deepened and he shook his head. He shouldn't grouse and give her troubles. He smiled at her. "How are you feeling?"

"Oh, I'm very well," she said. "You needn't worry yourself."

"I should and I will, we both know it." They held glances for a moment and then it became too oppressive. He looked toward the women at the window again. "And so all of Miss Westinghouse's family is now here with us."

His mother followed his stare. "Indeed. Alice's sister is a lovely woman, don't you think? It's clear they are very close, despite Lady Westinghouse's little comments to the contrary."

George let out a long sigh. His future mother-in-law was another issue entirely. The widowed viscountess could be severe with her daughter, and was a gossip when it came to anyone else. Including her stepdaughter. George mostly blocked it out, but he wasn't immune to facts.

"The woman is lovely, there is no denying that," George mused softly as Mrs. Manning brushed a lock of dark hair away from her cheek gently and smiled at her sister as she bubbled away.

"And she's so warm," his mother continued.

George arched a brow at that. Mrs. Manning had exhibited none of that warmth toward him, but he didn't say it. What would be the point? It would only trouble his mother more and he didn't want to add strain to her at present.

"They do seem close," George said, and tried to think if he'd ever heard his fiancée speak to him with any detail about her sister before. She must have, but he couldn't recall. That was often the way of their conversations, unfortunately. They were pleasant enough, but never stuck out in his mind. Sometimes it felt like they were both just trying to get through them and move on.

God, the idea that this would be the rest of his life was like a vise around his chest. He had to try harder. Had to do better and forget the past. Especially the recent past that had been distracting him the last few days. Thoughts of a woman in a mask, arched beneath him in shattering release.

"No," he muttered, and his mother tilted her head.

"What was that, dearest?"

"Nothing, Mama. Just woolgathering," he said with a shake of his head.

His mother's brow wrinkled, but then she released his arm and moved toward Miss Westinghouse and Mrs. Manning. "You must be so tired from your travels, Mrs. Manning. May I have someone show you to your chamber to let you rest?"

Unlike with him, Mrs. Manning did show enormous warmth toward his mother as she stepped away from her sister. "Oh, thank you, Lady Pembrooke. I do admit I could use a moment." She gave George the slight glance, but immediately drew it away. "Though I do look forward to our families forming even closer bonds during the next few weeks before the...the happy day of the wedding."

Her voice wavered a little on the word *happy*. It was almost imperceptible, but George noted it.

"As do we all," Clarissa said, coming to take Mrs. Manning's hand and give it a squeeze.

He knew his cousin well and it was obvious she liked Mrs. Manning. Normally that would be enough for him to judge her as worthy. And yet there was something troubled between them when there shouldn't be.

His mother went to the door and rang the bell. A maid appeared almost instantly and was given instructions to take Mrs. Manning to her chamber. She gave smiles all around until she reached George, then she barely inclined her head and rushed from the room.

He shook his head before the rest started to depart, separating off to do whatever they would do until supper. He moved to the window where Mrs. Manning had been standing and looked out on the same vista she had been examining. There had to be a reason she was so odd with him. He intended to find out what it was, if only for the sake of the marriage that was coming. It wouldn't do to have this woman dislike him, and he'd always been adept at bringing others to his side. He'd figure out a way to charm her.

CHAPTER 5

Lily thanked the servant who had brought her to her chamber, closed the door behind her and then rushed to the bedroom attached to the small antechamber. She gripped the edge of the bed as the tears she had been barely managing to hold back during the tea rolled down her cheeks. She could hardly breathe as she sobbed, her mind racing with such horrible, heartbreaking thoughts.

"H-how could it be h-him?" she asked herself out loud, her breath hiccupping out and garbling the words. "Oh-oh God, wh-why did it have to be *him?*"

She adored her sister beyond measure. Her entire life she had only ever wanted to protect Alice from pain, from loss, from sorrow. She'd put herself in front of her sister to keep her from harm and had kept secrets about her own life so that Alice didn't have to take in Lily's grief.

And now she had done *this.*

It didn't matter that she hadn't known. It didn't matter that the man, himself, didn't seem to recognize her thanks to the mask she had worn that night. That thought that he wouldn't just *know* her stung, but she pushed the pain away. She had no right to want him to know. To want him to remember her with the same searing, visceral desire that she had experienced in that blinding moment when he entered the chamber.

Should she confess? That thought made her entire body tremble and she shook her head. No. It was better this way. If he didn't know she was his masked lover, that meant she could keep it a secret. Nothing would have to change, nothing would have to be damaged thanks to her reckless, wanton behavior. In order to keep the truth from coming out, she would simply stay away from him entirely.

Only, her hesitations about his intentions for his marriage with her sister remained. In fact, they were stronger than ever. After all, a mere month before he was to wed Alice he had so passionately bedded another woman? If she wasn't the woman in question and had found out the truth, would she let that stand? Shouldn't she probe the matter further and be certain her sister would be well in her future?

Her mind spun at these disparate needs. Protection of herself versus protection of her sister. Could she do both? Her breath began to slow, but it still shook and the tears still trickled down her cheeks. Still, she was beginning to be able to think again. Somehow there had to be a way to probe Lockhart's intentions while keeping the truth of their night together tucked away.

Even if it haunted her. She had hoped for a night with no consequences and instead now there was this.

"No," she murmured, and rested her head against the bed, emotions only rolling harder in her chest.

In the outer chamber, she heard the door open and jolted back upright, wiping her tears away on the back of her hand as she heard her sister's voice.

"Oh, Lily I'm so glad you're here!" Alice said as she entered the bedroom and enveloped Lily in another tight hug. Happily, she didn't seem to notice Lily's emotional state as she began to flit around the room, looking at the labels on the bottles Susan had arranged on the dressing table and peeking into the wardrobe at the gowns hung there. "I have missed you so."

Lily pushed her thoughts of Lockhart away, deep down, praying they would stop intruding on everything. She needed to focus on Alice, now more than ever. "I have missed you, too, sweet," she said.

Alice twirled around to face her. "The last six months have been torture. All I wanted was you. I kept trying to make Mama let me see you, but you know her. She gave me excuse after excuse, telling me I had to focus on the future, not the past. As if you and I could ever be truly parted."

Lily pursed her lips. She had known the viscountess was manipulating the relationship but to hear the details still stung. "I'm surprised she allowed you to come to me now."

Alice shrugged. "She was *desperate* to connect herself more with the Earl and Countess of Kirkwood and I took the opportunity to slip away so we could have a moment in private."

"Hmmm," Lily mused, keeping her thoughts on that subject to herself. Prudence had always been grasping. "How is she being with...with you?"

Now her sister's expression fell slightly and some of the exuberance left her. "You know. She's being *Mama*. Trying to manage every aspect of my engagement to Lockhart."

Once again, visions of Lockhart's face swarmed Lily's mind. His expression as he watched her in the parlor. His expression as he watched her while he perched between her legs, wicked tongue bringing such pleasure.

She gasped at the invading images and pivoted away. "H-how so?"

"She keeps trying to push me to exhibit more for the family. Trying to raise me up on some pedestal. And she's *always* trying to make me talk to Lockhart." Alice shook her head as if the idea was ludicrous. "Thank goodness Mary is here. She's my only saving grace."

Lily wrinkled her brow. "Your maid?"

Alice worried her lip a moment and then nodded. "Yes."

Lily shifted slightly. "I admit I was surprised when you chose Mary to be your maid when you came of age. I thought you'd want someone with more experience, especially as you'll be entering such an elevated house. Mary is so young."

"We're the same age. I suppose we'll grow together." Alice sounded wistful, but then she refocused on Lily. "But enough about that. Now that you've met him, what do you think of Lockhart?"

Just his name set off another torrent of reaction that Lily couldn't control. His hands. His mouth. His gentle voice after he'd shattered her world into rainbows and then talked to her afterward like they were truly connected. How much that had meant to her.

"He's very handsome," she managed to gasp out.

Alice's brow wrinkled. "I...I suppose."

Lily's eyes went wide. Whatever else Alice thought of the man she would marry, certainly his physical attractiveness wasn't up for debate. How could anyone not look at him and be immediately drawn in by all his angles and curves?

Alice sighed. "I should go before Mama comes looking for me. I'll see you at supper?"

Lily dropped her gaze. Sharing tea with Lockhart had been nearly impossible, she wasn't certain she could manage an entire meal with him just down the table from her. Or God, perhaps even close to her. What if he tried to talk to her? What if she couldn't school her expressions and he would guess, at last, her true identity? He was an observant man, after all. No fool.

"I-I am very tired," she said. "I wonder if I should skip supper tonight so I can be my best the next time I'm gathered with all your future family."

"Oh." Alice looked a little upset, but then she nodded. "Of course, Lily. I know you must be exhausted, especially after the troubles on the road. I'll make your excuses with the countess and I know she'll understand. She's so very kind."

"Thank you, love," Lily said, and smiled as her sister hugged her again and then hustled from the room, off to give excuses and then probably go dance on flower petals like the sprite she was.

When she was gone, Lily flopped back on her bed and put her arms over her face. At least she'd given herself some time to figure out what to do. How to act. How to breathe when she was in the same room with her sister's fiancé. The surprise of his identity would be faded by tomorrow when she'd have to face him again. Certainly, she could pull herself together.

And also refocus on Alice. Protecting her was the most important thing now. She couldn't stray from that path just because Lockhart existed and what they'd shared had happened. In fact, she had to rededicate herself to her sisterly role even more just to be certain Alice was in good hands.

She could do all that and also make sure no one ever found out what she'd done. Especially the man she'd done it with.

~

George stood in the parlor at seven-thirty, drink in hand, and he found himself watching the door. He could have pretended otherwise, but he was fully aware he was waiting for the only person who had not yet joined their party: Mrs. Manning. Truth be told, he was beginning to become bothered that she wasn't there yet.

"We're missing your sister, Miss Westinghouse," he said with a brief glance at his fiancée, who stood at his side, watching the others as they talked and sipped their drinks.

She started a fraction and looked up at him almost as if she forgot he existed and then inclined her head. "My sister won't be joining us, my lord. I'm so sorry I didn't mention it earlier. I fear she's very tired from the road and needed a little extra rest."

"Ah," he said. "Of course, that makes perfect sense. Travel can be most taxing."

There was a flicker of disappointment at that information, but he pushed it aside. He only wanted to get to the work of understanding *why* the woman seemed so distant from him when she seemed perfectly at ease with everyone else in the house. He had no other reason to be interested in Mrs. Manning's comings and goings.

He drew a breath and refocused his attention where it should be: on his fiancée. She really was very pretty with her perfectly curled blonde hair and blue eyes, both so different from her sister. He should have felt some stirring for her, but he didn't.

His mind drifted briefly to the woman from the hell a few days before. Of her ardor when they kissed, of the ripple of her when she came apart beneath his tongue and cock. Of how fucking good she felt in his arms afterward.

He blinked. *That* was an entirely inappropriate thought to be having while standing next to his future bride. He was normally much better at separating the proper world from the wicked one he loved to visit. Why couldn't he do it now?

"You—you must be pleased to have Mrs. Manning here," he choked out, if only to force himself to stop thinking.

To his surprise, Miss Westinghouse lit up in a way she'd never done before in any conversation with him. She pivoted more fully toward him, clasped her hands together and said, "Oh, yes! I do adore seeing her. She is my favorite person in the world…well, *almost* my favorite. Lily is almost ten years my elder, so she was a second mother to me as I grew up. I couldn't love her more."

"How wonderful," he said, and meant it. He had been an only child and had often wished he could have had the closeness of that kind of relationship with a brother or sister. He had something like it with Clarissa, but it wasn't really the same between cousins, as they didn't live in the same house. "And your mother must be happy to have her here, as well."

He didn't know exactly why he said that, for he had been reminded by his mother earlier in the day that Lady Westinghouse's relationship to her stepdaughter was *not* close, but he supposed he wanted to know more about that fact. This slip was one way to force the subject.

Miss Westinghouse's expression fluttered slightly, some of her excitement immediately tempered by whatever thoughts his comment created. "Well, er, she isn't Lily's mother, you know. "

"Ah yes, that's right. I'd forgotten."

Alice nodded. "Mama married our father only a few months after the first viscountess's death."

George lifted his brows. A few *months*. He couldn't imagine how he would feel if his father did the same thing after the death of his mother. His chest hurt just thinking about it. No wonder the two women had some tension between them.

"I do wish they were closer, but…" Miss Westinghouse trailed off and blushed. "Forgive me."

He shook his head. "There's nothing to forgive. I asked the question and I wanted the answer. Soon our families will be linked by our marriage. I'd be remiss if I didn't try to make some understanding of yours."

She worried her lip and then sighed before she continued, "I suppose you're right. You must understand that the trouble isn't on Lily's side. My sister is the kindest, most wonderful person I know. I adore her beyond what I could ever express."

George took in that information. It was interesting that Miss Westinghouse would rather he think ill of her mother than her sister. It truly did speak to their strong bond. And made him more determined than ever to get to the bottom of the coldness Mrs. Manning had exhibited toward him earlier in the day. With a start, he realized Miss Westinghouse was still speaking.

"And I hope—" She broke up and looked fully into his eyes for what he realized was the first time. "I do hope that she'll be welcome in our home."

"Of course." He said it without hesitation. Even if Mrs. Manning despised him, even if he never understood why or changed those thoughts, he would never deny his wife the pleasure of the company of her sister. That seemed cruel beyond measure. He might be a great many things, but he never wanted to be cruel.

Miss Westinghouse let out a shaky sigh and he could see the relief wash over her face. "That's wonderful. Thank you, Lockhart. And I'm certain you two will be friends, as well. No one could know Lily and not love her."

He wasn't at all certain of that fact yet, but he smiled nonetheless to further comfort her. "I'll do my best, Miss Westinghouse."

"My lords and ladies, supper is served," Reeves intoned from the door, an interruption to the conversation.

George held out an elbow to Miss Westinghouse and she took it. He frowned, for once again there was no physical reaction in him at all to her touch, despite a conversation that was far more personal than any they'd ever shared before. Still he had to hope they were on the right track now. And he would just have to try harder to make himself feel something for her.

It was the only way.

CHAPTER 6

Lily hadn't slept more than a few restless hours the night before. Instead, she had tossed and turned, thoughts racing through her mind, heartbreaking pain threatening to crush her.

And when she *had* managed to drift off? She'd dreamed the same dreams she'd been having since the night of the Donville Masquerade. She'd dreamed of *him*. His low voice in her ear, his hands on her, his mouth on her, only this time he wasn't her fantasy Ares, he was Lockhart. And he was clean shaven, his hair trimmed, every inch the very man who was just down the hallway from her now.

Dreams that had once been erotic and pleasing for her had now woken her bolt upright, sweaty with desire and shaking with self-loathing for the same.

She'd risen at dawn, calling for Susan to ready her, and now, a few hours later, she roamed the still manor house, trying to find some way to forget what she'd done.

The calm and beauty of the home around her certainly helped. There was a quiet sophistication to these halls, with their richly painted or tapestried walls, fine artwork mixed with portraits of ancient family faces and modern furniture pieces. No one who visited here would doubt they were amongst important people with a long history of power and influence.

But there was also warmth to be found in tiny details in the chambers. There was a well-worn chair in one of the parlors with a half-finished needlepoint set on its arm. Was it Lady Kirkwood's, brought to help pass her time here while she celebrated her cousin's wedding? Or perhaps it belonged to Lady Pembrooke. She would have to ask later, as she also enjoyed the pastime and she wished to compliment the owner of the piece. It was so neat and finely done.

On a mantel in another room was a pretty cigar box, engraved with a flourished *P*. Certainly that was Lord Pembrooke's since she didn't recall the smell or taste of cigar smoke on Lockhart. She could imagine the older earl standing there as he watched over his family, puffing his cigar.

There were miniatures beneath glass in another room. She thought perhaps they were displayed this way purposefully, for when travelers inquired with the house staff for a tour when the family wasn't in residence. Certainly, anyone in the county would want a glimpse of this fine place. And yet the miniatures were so lively. Lord and Lady Pembrooke were displayed, an image from years ago, perhaps even painted when they were first engaged. Each little painting faced the other, as if the couple were staring into each other's eyes.

Then there was a miniature of who Lily believed was Lady Kirkwood, as a young girl. She truly was a favorite cousin to be held at the same level as the rest of the family. And next to her was one of Lockhart. Despite the picture being from his youth, there was no mistaking those startling eyes or the hint of a wicked smile on those lips. When this was painted had he already visited the Donville Masquerade for the first time? Was he already on the path that would inevitably lead him to her?

She shook her head. Why did every single moment have to drag her back to that one? This tour was meant to stop these feelings, not stoke them.

At any rate, those little details helped her feel the beating heart of the family that sometimes was hidden in the pretentious lines of the Upper Ten Thousand. Including her own. Her father and Prudence had been careful about public perception. Perhaps because their quick marriage after her mother's death had caused a bit of a scandal when it happened. As a result, they never left anything real out for others to see.

She sighed as she turned yet another corner and found herself face-to-face with Lady Kirkwood, who was coming from the other direction.

"Oh, Mrs. Manning!" the countess said with a wide smile. "Good morning."

"My lady," Lily returned with a respectful incline of her head. Here she had been so looking forward to meeting this woman, who was a friend to Esme and her sister-in-law Marianne. Now she could only worry what Lockhart's cousin would think of her if she knew the truth. This stolen night had a ripple effect that Lily supposed she deserved.

"You look as though you had a restful night. We missed you at supper." Lady Kirkwood stepped closer with a genuine smile.

Lily's cheeks grew hot with embarrassment. "I do apologize for my absence."

She said nothing more for she didn't want to lie to this woman's face and she certainly couldn't tell her the truth of why she'd fled the Lockhart's company. The reaction to that would be something to behold, she had no doubt. Even Lady Kirkwood's friendship with Esme wouldn't protect her from this woman's disgust at what Lily had done.

The other woman examined her a moment, her brow furrowing slightly, but she didn't press the issue further. "Are you taking a tour of the estate?"

"A little self-guided one, yes," Lily said. "I saw a pretty needlepoint in one of the parlors. Was it yours?"

"Oh, heavens no," Clarissa said. "I do needlepoint, of course. A lady always should, I was taught. But it must belong to my aunt. She's a marvel."

Lily nodded. "She truly is, and I shall tell her so when next I see her. The piece was wonderful. As is the house."

"It is," Lady Kirkwood agreed with a sigh of pleasure. "I did adore the times we came here when I was a child."

"Yes, my sister tells me you are very close your aunt and uncle and…and Lockhart."

Lady Kirkwood's expression lit up with genuine love. "I am. They were a warm light in what was occasionally a very chilly world. My aunt is the kindest woman I know, my uncle has more heart under that gruff exterior than perhaps he's given credit for. And my cousin is like a brother to me. I could not adore George more."

"High praise, indeed," Lily said softly.

"Have you explored the gardens yet?"

"No," Lily admitted. "I wasn't sure the best exit to use to get there."

Lady Kirkwood offered her arm. "Then let me take you. It will be beautiful this time of day."

Lily smiled as she took the woman's elbow. It was impossible not to like her, for she was so kind. "Thank you, Lady Kirkwood."

"Oh, please call me Clarissa," she insisted. "I know it isn't entirely proper, but we're to be family very soon. It seems silly to worry too much about that. Besides, I know you're already such good friends with dearest Esme that I cannot imagine we won't be drawn together a good deal after the wedding."

Lily swallowed at that thought. It was wonderful to think she could be good friends with this woman, that had been the attraction of this meeting, after all. But the idea that they would see each other a great deal was based on the fact that Lily would be part of Alice's new family. With Lockhart. And that was a situation too fraught to be borne at present.

They walked through a few more twisting turns of the big home and finally into a quiet, dim ballroom. Clarissa gave her a little smile. "I take us through the ballroom because it has the best view of the garden from its terrace."

She pushed open a set of double glass doors and sunshine hit Lily in the face, warming her skin immediately. The terrace behind the ballroom was an enormous, stone parapet with a wrought iron balcony wall. They stepped up to it together and Lily caught her breath. The garden below was as beautiful as Clarissa had described. It was a neatly trimmed mass of bright green hedges mixed with a rainbow cacophony of beautiful flowers of all kinds.

"Oh my!" she breathed and all her tangled thoughts seemed to ease for just a moment.

"Isn't it something?" Clarissa asked with a wide smile. "Oh, I could get lost here. I certainly did as a child, often on purpose. I will say that Kirkwood's garden in London and his country estate is equally beautiful. I've taken a keen interest in the maintenance of both since our marriage. I want them each to feel as lush and wonderful as this place and he supports that fully."

Lily gave her a side glance as they walked to a spot in the terrace that allowed one to come down a set of stone stairs to the garden itself. "Forgive my saying so, but one only has to look at you two together to guess that Kirkwood would support you if you said you wished to join the circus."

Clarissa laughed long and hard. "What a concept! He would be mightily shocked by such a thing, especially given our beginnings, but yes. The man would support anything I wished to do. He is remarkable."

Lily smiled. They were one more couple deeply in love, it seemed. And it was both wonderful to see and painful, both because her own marriage had been so far from that truth and she feared Alice's would be no better.

"Oh my, look at these begonias!" Clarissa said as she released Lily and moved forward to the plants just off the crushed stone path. "They must have just bloomed."

Pushing her thoughts away, Lily joined Clarissa and for a little while simply allowed herself to enjoy the countess's deep knowledge of flowers and plants. It was a subject the other woman was clearly deeply passionate about and it was impossible not to be swept up in her enthusiasm. Lily was beginning to relax for the first time since Lockhart had revealed himself the day before when Clarissa turned away from the plant they were examining and let out a little gasp.

Lily turned to look at what had caught her attention only to find Lockhart, himself, walking down the path toward them. His head was down and he didn't seem to have noticed them yet.

Lily's first instinct was to run. Or to hide behind the nearest obliging tree trunk. But Clarissa obviously knew none of those impulses and she stepped forward and called out to him.

"George, that cannot be you," she said, her voice heavy with playful teasing. "I must be dreaming."

He lifted his gaze and grinned as he noticed his cousin. Lily caught her breath at that smile, which seemed to light up the garden just as much as the sun. It put her to mind of his wicked grin when he touched her at the hell. She shook away those thoughts and all the reactions her traitorous body experienced with them.

His eyes moved to her and the smile dimmed a little. "Why, if it isn't my favorite cousin. Good morning, Clarissa. Mrs. Manning."

Lily couldn't quite manage to speak, but inclined her head in a faint attempt to be polite.

"You must forgive my shock," Clarissa said, this time to her. "But my cousin is *never* an early riser. He thinks it is as unforgivable as my own husband does." She winked at George playfully before she added, "You know the reputation of rakes: layabout scoundrels, all of them."

Lily pursed her lips, her mind floating to Alice again. To her future. Lockhart glanced at her and chuckled, but it seemed forced. "Come now, Clarissa, Mrs. Manning will believe you."

"Lily *should* believe me," Clarissa insisted, her tone still laced with teasing. "The stories I could tell you about this man and his ways. I'm certain my husband could tell even worse ones."

"I'm sure," Lily said, dropping her eyes away from Lockhart. When he looked at her, her mind wanted to wander to inappropriate places.

"I will pay you ten pounds to keep your secrets, cousin," Lockhart said.

Clarissa laughed. "A hearty sum. You must fear what I would reveal. I'll consider your offer, George, and be back to negotiate later."

"Very good." Lockhart shifted. "Er, so you're enjoying the garden this morning, I see."

"Yes, Aunt Louisa's begonias have bloomed beautifully, perhaps overnight. I'll have to tell her and bring her down to look at them later."

From the corner of her eye, Lily saw a flutter of something work over Lockhart's face at the mention of his mother. Some worry, perhaps a little pain.

She found herself wondering about it, even though his tone was neutral as he said, "She'd love that. You two green thumbs can talk gardens for hours." He glanced up at the house. "I believe breakfast will be served soon. Might I return with you?"

"Please," Clarissa said, motioning him to join them.

Lily stiffened. It seemed there was no escaping this now. She would simply have to ensure he didn't recognize her. Not that he appeared to have any ability to do so. She had been, it seemed, utterly forgettable to him, and not just because she'd worn a mask. He didn't recognize her eyes or her voice, nor the way she moved, nothing at all.

Which made her wonder how many women had been had and forgotten by him. And what did that mean for her sister's future? Or at least that's what she tried to wonder rather than allow for sharp jealousy at the thought. She had no right to it.

She drew a breath and began to walk with the two of them up

the path, hoping Lockhart would stay focused on his cousin rather than her. It didn't seem to be in the cards, though, for he leaned around Clarissa slightly and said, "I must say, Mrs. Manning, your sister speaks very highly of you."

Lily wondered what Alice would say if she knew the tangled truth, but kept her eyes on the path. "Oh, that's lovely. I do adore Alice."

Both Clarissa and Lockhart seemed to be waiting for her add more to that statement and normally she would have, but this time she kept her thoughts to herself. Lockhart did not appear to be deterred by her silence. "You two grew up in Briar Grange, yes? Out in Sussex?"

Lily pursed her lips, both happy and horrible memories of her home flooding her. "We did."

Now Lily felt him staring at her and realized Clarissa was, as well. Her short answers seemed to surprise them both and why wouldn't they? It was bordering on impolite and neither of them would understand why her attitude had suddenly changed after her friendliness toward Clarissa.

Happily they had reached the house now and quickly moved to the breakfast room where the others were beginning to gather, including Alice. She faced them both, still trying to keep her gaze from Lockhart's. "Thank you for the wonderful tour of the garden, Clarissa. And-and for your welcome company, my lord. Please excuse me. I'll join my sister."

She inclined her head and ducked away, feeling both their stares on her back as she did so. His gaze, especially, felt heavy on her and she let out a shaky breath as she reached Alice and greeted her. How in the world could she navigate this?

She had to figure it out. And soon.

~

It had been a few hours since George's encounter with Mrs. Manning...Lily, he was beginning to think of her as since everyone else seemed to call her that over and over. She was rather like a lily actually. Beautiful, startling and temperamental. He didn't understand her, nor her odd and almost hostile behavior toward him.

Even now as the company gathered in the parlor, drinking tea and playing cards, she seemed to look at anyone in the room but him. Like she was hiding, or at least trying to do so. But that only made him want to...to chase her. Find her. Uncover the secret of why.

The obvious answer would be Miss Westinghouse, of course. Lily obviously adored her younger sister, one only had to have eyes in their head to see that. And Miss Westinghouse had called her a second mother, so that meant she would be protective. It was likely the answer to his questions was that she doubted him and his intentions. And yet she made no effort to question him or ensure he was a good match. Perhaps it was up to him to answer for those unspoken hesitations, in order to put her at ease.

His mother stepped up then, thankfully interrupting his brood. "Are you so focused on your future bride then?"

He started. Lily *was* standing with Miss Westinghouse. He had hardly noticed his intended at her side. He glanced at his mother. "Just thinking," he said, dodging the question.

She held his gaze for a moment and then looked toward the two women, herself. "I couldn't help but note there is a little tension between you and Mrs. Manning."

He shrugged. There was no denying that fact to his mother. She was far too keen an observer to pretend facts away. "Yes, I've felt that too. I cannot imagine why she would think negatively toward me. I never met the woman before yesterday afternoon." He didn't add that it somehow felt like he *had* met her before. "I wonder if she doesn't approve the match for some reason."

His mother frowned deeply. "I hope that isn't true. She may have no say in the arrangements, but judging from your Alice's adoration of her sister, Mrs. Manning's opinions *could* influence her. It would behoove you to soften the woman to you. Perhaps show her that you have a care for Alice."

George almost laughed, for he didn't know how to prove something that felt so untrue. He wanted no harm to ever come to the young woman he would wed, he certainly wished her to be happy and knew that would be his duty in the future. But there was nothing beyond that, no matter how hard he hoped that would change. Lord knew he kept trying to summon a true care and could not.

"Yes," he managed to croak out.

His mother glanced at the women again and then nodded, as if she'd come to some decision. "I'll seat you next to Mrs. Manning at supper."

He jolted at the idea, but then nodded. "Er, yes. Good. And I will put on all my charm to change whatever poor opinion she may have of me."

"I'm certain you will," his mother said with a little dry smile. "I should have made your middle name Charming."

"Instead of Philip Peter Littleton," he said. "Honestly it would be less of a silly mouthful."

His mother laughed as she briefly rested her head on his arm. He slid that same arm around her and squeezed gently. She felt so small to him, thinner than usual. And this mattered to her. His future mattered. So he would do whatever he needed to do to make it happen the way she wished it to. Even if that meant overcoming whatever problem it was that plagued Lily Manning.

CHAPTER 7

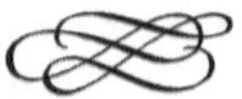

After just a full day at Pembrooke Hills, Lily had never felt
more anxious to have additional guests arrive to a gathering.
Not only would they provide a much-needed buffer between herself
and Lockhart, but she knew she'd feel her own status less keenly
with more people around. At present, she was the only attendee
beyond her stepmother who was not attached. That meant she had
to stand beside Prudence far too often as the couples paired off.

Even now, as the pre-supper drinks drained away and the butler
came in to announce the meal was ready, Prudence stepped to Lily's
side to await their time to enter the dining room together.

"That is a very pretty dress, Prudence," Lily said, attempting the
kindness she always did when it came to the viscountess.

Prudence sniffed and her voice was strained as she said, "Thank
you. You know, I see what you are doing."

Lily turned toward her slightly. "Doing?" she repeated, her heart
beginning to throb a little faster. The last person she wanted to
know the truth was Prudence. If somehow she had guessed—

"You are making yourself the center of the party," Prudence clar-
ified with a little glare. "Acting as though *you* are the one more
attached to Alice, when *I* am her mother."

Lily sighed. Over the years, she and Prudence had often exchanged words about this very topic. Her stepmother refused to acknowledge that she had not very much interest in Alice until she could start making arrangements for her good marriage. And that Lily had taken up the role of mother even though for many years she was just a child herself. When she was reminded of that fact? Well, punishment often followed, even when Lily no longer lived within her stepmother's walls.

The latest version of that had been keeping Alice from her. When she'd been cut off from sister in the last six months, hearing of her life and her engagement only through letters, it had been like having a part of her heart torn away.

"We are all here to celebrate my sister and help her prepare for what I hope will be a very happy future," Lily said, meeting Prudence's eyes evenly. "*That* is all I care about."

Prudence drew a breath as if she was going to continue speaking, but the group was moving and it had become time for them to join in it. They fell into step and Lily could feel her stepmother seething, though she said nothing else and merely flounced off to her place at the table when they reached the dining room. She didn't even say a farewell.

Lily was pleased that she wouldn't be near her that night, but as she reached the seat the footman had indicated to her, those happy feelings faded, for standing next to her chair, holding it out for her, was Lockhart.

He smiled at her and her heart thudded despite all attempts to be unmoved by him. "Good evening, Mrs. Manning. I am so glad we're seated next to each other."

The tenor of his voice made its way down her spine and she couldn't breathe as memories threatened to mob her yet again. She shut her eyes, willing his husky moans of a very different kind of pleasure to leave her mind.

"Mrs. Manning?" he repeated, and there was concern in that voice now.

She opened her eyes and gasped out, "Are you? Why?"

His slight recoil at her sharpness was exactly what she didn't want. It would only draw his attention to her all the more. Oh, why couldn't she control herself when she was around him? Why did she keep making all her tangled thoughts more obvious, not less?

She straightened her spine, smoothed her skirt and took the seat he was still waiting for her to fill. He took his own beside her and turned slightly to continue their conversation. "Because I wish to get to know you better. I'm to marry your sister, after all, and you obviously mean a great deal to her."

Lily looked down the table toward where Alice was seated near Lord and Lady Pembrooke, talking to them softly, a warm smile on her pretty face.

She sighed. "As she does to me."

When she dared to look back at Lockhart, he was examining her face. She dropped her gaze, hoping he wouldn't see anything he recognized. At least at present she was the only one carrying this horrible secret. If he realized the truth, she might expire on the spot.

"I must say, I'm surprised we never crossed paths before now. Alice tells me we are of an age," he said as the first course was laid out before them.

She almost laughed, though there was no pleasure to be had at that observation. What *would* he say if he knew exactly how and where their paths *had* crossed? Or would he think nothing of it? Was his reputation as a rake so true that he would care little for what they'd done? For how it might affect Alice?

Before she'd known who he was, how they knew each other, she had already worried about his man. Whatever else had transpired a few days ago in London, did she not still owe it to Alice to ask questions and make observations about him, his intentions and his ability to feel? After all, she knew the consequences of an arranged marriage when it went wrong.

She cleared her throat after she took a few bites of food that she didn't even taste. "Well, my lord, I was married, of course. And I moved in the circles of my husband. Thomas was much older."

His brows lifted in what appeared to be surprise. "Thomas Manning?"

She nodded.

"I hadn't made the connection." He seemed briefly troubled by that, but then he seemed to shake that reaction off. "Yes, he was a distant friend of my father's from his youth rather than my own. Their fathers were friends, I think."

She thought of Viscount Manning, her late husband's father. A nasty man who had died almost immediately upon her marriage. His elder son had taken the title and Thomas had been locked out of whatever he hoped to receive from the estate beyond a living. But that had never been enough and it had only made him more bitter and cold, especially as she failed to produce heirs he might use to his advantage.

She shrugged, willing herself to push those memories aside and he continued, "It makes sense then, that we would move in different circles."

"And then when he died I was, of course, in mourning," she continued. She didn't add that she had never mourned her husband in truth. That she'd felt a wicked sense of freedom rather than sorrow. Certainly she couldn't add how she'd judged herself for those awful feelings for months.

The woman she'd been at the Donville Masquerade might have told her gentle, passionate lover such a thing. She might have let her Ares in and allowed him to comfort her. But here? No. That would be entirely inappropriate.

"My condolences," he said softly.

She pursed her lips. "Thank you."

She looked at him once more instead of dodging her gaze away. Lord, he was beautiful. How could a man be so beautiful with all those angles, how could he look so proper when he was clearly built for passion and sin under those perfectly pressed clothes?

She shook her head. This needed to stop. "And what about you, my lord? What secrets do *you* have to reveal?"

"Secrets?" he repeated. There was a hesitation in the conversation as the empty plates were drawn away and replaced. Normally Lily would have enjoyed the surprise of whatever dish came next, but at present she didn't even notice the supper. As the servant stepped away he continued, "Is that what we're exchanging here?"

"Facts then," she said, happy that her tone could be cool, at least, when everything else felt close and hot and dizzying. "That is how people get to know each other, after all."

"That sounds very efficient." He smiled slightly. "So what *facts* do you wish to know, Mrs. Manning?"

She looked at Alice again. Her sister had glanced down the table at Lily and Lockhart and there was sadness on her face. Worry. Girding herself, Lily set her fork down on the edge of her plate and said, "I suppose I wonder what a man of your age and reputation finds of interest in my innocent sister."

~

George nearly choked on his bite of food at the intensity of Lily's question. He set his own cutlery down and tilted his head. "That is…that is direct."

She shrugged. "We have little time until you two wed. And I'm not the sort of person who dodges important topics." She flushed. "Not usually, at any rate."

"And here I thought you'd question me about books or my favorite country dance," he said, hoping the quip would melt some of her ice. It didn't. She didn't laugh or smile, just continued to watch him with those bright brown eyes that seemed to catch a man and yank him forward even if he didn't wish to be there. He cleared his throat. "Obviously you have serious concerns about this union."

"I do." She looked away from him, as she always seemed to do when they were too close either physically or when they began to understand each other in even the slightest way.

He nodded. So all his fears were correct, then. "Well, I'd like to address them, but perhaps not at the family supper table."

She jerked her face up and glanced around, as if recalling exactly where they were. Heat suffused her cheeks, bringing attention to high cheekbones. She truly had the most fascinating face.

"Yes, of course. Forgive me, my lord," she said softly.

"Perhaps we could discuss it later," he said, wanting her to know he was willing to speak to her, that he wasn't just trying to put her off. As much as he wanted to do just that, how could he? "In the meantime, perhaps you'd like to know my thoughts on art?"

She shifted a little and glanced at him. "Well, I suppose it wouldn't hurt. I did notice your family home has some wonderful pieces by artists I've only ever seen in museums."

He smiled at her response, at the quiet thrill of her words. So, she *could* be cracked. Which meant he might be able to ease her fears. Later, when they could have privacy so he could do just that.

Lily stood by herself in the parlor, sipping her sherry as she pondered the night. Despite herself, she had enjoyed Lockhart's company at supper. She found him to be educated, focused and his charisma was impossible to deny. He could easily discuss her favorite artists and then shift to current events of the day. He might make a quip that made the room smile or ask a question that truly seemed to focus in on who a person was.

She had evaded all those types of questions, of course, because the last thing she could allow him to do was see her. Not the truth of her. Not ever.

To her surprise, she felt a hand slide through her elbow and she jumped as she realized Alice had crossed the room and joined her. Her sister rested her head on Lily's shoulder for a moment and then she looked up at her. "You and Lockhart seemed to be involved in deep conversation at supper. Did you have a good talk?"

Lily flinched. "We—we did," she said, and added nothing more.

Alice didn't seem to care that she didn't expound on the topic, she merely looked thrilled. Relieved. Why so relieved? As if Lily could save her somehow. It was intensely troubling.

As was the fact that when she looked across the room she found Lockhart watching her. Not her sister, not them as a pair: her. His gray-blue gaze flitted over her briefly and then returned to Clarissa and Lord Kirkwood as the threesome talked.

"Alice," Prudence said sharply as she joined the two. Alice's hand tightened on Lily's arm for a fraction of a moment before she smiled at her mother.

"Yes, Mama?"

"You should play." Prudence pointed to the Broadwood Grand in the corner of the parlor.

"Oh." Alice looked toward the beautiful piano with a covetous gaze. She had always loved to play. "Oh, yes! And Lily, you and Lockhart should dance."

Before Lily could find a way out of that, Prudence grabbed her arm, fingers digging into her skin. "Not tonight, dearest. Now go."

Alice slipped off and Prudence faced Lily. "*This* is exactly what I'm talking about."

"What?"

"Dancing with your sister's intended?" Prudence tilted her head as if that proved any accusation that could ever be made.

Lily threw her hands up, but she kept her tone soft so no one else would be drawn into this ridiculous argument. Well, she wished it was entirely ridiculous. Prudence was closer to the mark than she knew. "*Alice* is the one who asked me to dance with her fiancé. It wasn't and would never be my idea." She clenched her teeth. "As I said before supper, my *only* desire in being here is to protect my sister from *anyone* who might threaten her well-being."

Prudence folded her arms. "That isn't your duty."

"Oh, yes, it is. It always has been." Lily didn't wait for a response, but stepped away toward the set of double doors that led from the parlor to a small terrace.

She sucked in the cool night air, trying to calm herself. It was impossible, though. She would not be calm when she was here, that was evident. There was too much at stake, too much to hide. Too much to hate herself over.

She heard the terrace doors reopen and close behind her and pivoted, expecting to see Prudence coming out to continue to harangue her. The truth was far worse. It was Lockhart who stood there, bathed in moonlight, watching her for a moment before he stepped forward.

"Mrs. Manning, are you well?" he asked.

"I'm fine," she snapped, turning away from him, praying he would not come closer. But he did. She caught a whiff of that wonderful, masculine scent of him and her knees weakened a little. What would he taste like tonight if she kissed him? Would he still feel like Ares, or something different?

"Forgive me, but I don't think you are," he said. "You appear upset. Aside from a handful of times when you've been away from the group with Miss Westinghouse, you've *been* upset since your arrival. Please, won't you let me be of some assistance?"

She glanced at him over her shoulder. He looked so sincere in his desire to fix things that for a moment, she considered confessing. Telling him who she was and why she was feeling this way and trying to find some way for them to work it out together. But that was the way of a fool. It would only make things worse, that was certain.

So she folded her arms instead. "Please, my lord, don't press this."

"How can I not?" He moved closer. "Especially if *I* have any part in your pain."

"You?" she sputtered. "Why would you think that?"

He shrugged. "I have eyes in my head. I have sense, though some might debate that."

She stared at him a fraction of a moment more and then shook her head. "There's nothing you can do, Lockhart."

She turned away from him, back toward the house.

"Wait," she heard him say, but she didn't stop. She slipped back into the parlor, past the talking guests and her glaring stepmother, and left without another word.

She had to get upstairs where no one would bother her. And she had to somehow get a handle on her emotions. Because at present she was heading down a hill that could only result in a huge crash and destruction.

And not just for her.

George stood in a parlor the next morning with troubling thoughts passing through his mind. Thoughts of a woman, but not his fiancée. No, he couldn't stop thinking of Lily Manning.

The woman vexed him, that was certain. He wanted to tell himself that it was just because of her unexplained reactions to him, and that *was* part of the issue. But the other was…something else. He couldn't stop thinking of her broken expression on the terrace the night before when she'd all but begged him to leave her be. He couldn't stop thinking of her smile, the one she easily bestowed on every person in this house but him.

He couldn't stop thinking of the fact that his erotic dreams, the ones that had starred the woman from the Donville Masquerade over the last week, now always transformed into her.

He truly was a bastard.

"Brooding, are we?"

George turned and forced a smile as Kirkwood entered the chamber. "You know me, I never brood."

Kirkwood's brow wrinkled and his teasing expression swiftly transformed to one of concern. Fuck, that was no good. His friend would chew on this now like a dog with a bone and there was no way George could explain what was happening in his body and heart. He didn't fully understand it, himself.

"What's going on with you?" Kirkwood asked.

Turning back to the window, George sighed. "I don't know what you mean."

There was a long enough pause that he looked back over his shoulder to make sure his friend was still there. Kirkwood was, staring at him, arms folded. "When you told me you had decided to marry, that you had consented to the arrangement your mother made, I was concerned."

"Don't start," George muttered.

"I haven't, not in all these months," Kirkwood said. "Because you're a grown man and can usually be trusted to make your own decisions."

"Usually?" George repeated with a glare.

"Well, in this case, that ability is questionable. It becomes more and more questionable every time I see you with Alice. At first I could brush it off, call the awkwardness and distance between you the consequence of an arranged marriage. I suppose I hoped that you might over time find the same connection with your intended that I have with Clarissa despite *our* forced beginnings."

"You fell in love with my cousin and she with you and I couldn't be happier for you both. But that isn't always the way of these types of agreements," George said. "That reflects nothing on me and my ability to make decisions."

"I suppose it might not." Kirkwood's brow furrowed and his tone softened a little. It sounded a little like pity lacing the undeniable concern when he continued, "And yet this entire matter has been rushed. Like it's some race to hell for both of you. Meanwhile, you both look as though you're going to the gallows, not to a happy future together."

"You're being melodramatic," George muttered.

Kirkwood was undeterred. "Is there *any* connection at all between you and Alice?"

"You already reminded me, so I'll remind you in turn, there wasn't a connection between you and Clarissa initially, either, so you're one to talk," George snapped, perhaps more harshly than he meant to.

"But it wasn't like *this*." Kirkwood shook his head. "Clarissa frustrated and fascinated me. I wanted her and I *liked* her. The rest was there, I was just too stubborn to recognize it until it was all I could see."

George threw up his hands. "What do you want me to say? I'm sure there will be plenty of time in the many years ahead to get to know and appreciate Miss Westinghouse."

"And that, *Jesus*. What do you intend to call her when you can no longer hide behind *Miss Westinghouse*? Or will you switch to Lady Lockhart and eventually Lady Pembrooke? Over time will you forget she has a first name at all?"

George wanted to argue against this intrusion, but it was impossible when everything his friend was saying was true. Painfully, terrifyingly true. To the point that he found himself dreaming of masked women and his intended's own sister.

"What would you have me do?" he asked, and this time there was no heat to the question.

Kirkwood stepped closer. "I want one of my dearest friends not to be miserable. Partly because you are my wife's favorite cousin and it would break her heart for you to be so. And partly because I actually *like* you."

"A difficult admission, I'm certain," George said with a humorless laugh.

"Almost impossible to make."

He ran a hand through his hair. Kirkwood was his best friend. There was no denying him, even if George couldn't say everything that bubbled dangerously within his heart and mind. "It's-it's too late to change things now," he said slowly. "It is what it is."

The desperation that came along with those words nearly drowned George, but somehow he managed to stay upright.

"It won't be too late until you say I do before God and a church full of people." Kirkwood's tone was gentle even though his expression was lined with pain. Pain for *him*.

George ignored it. He couldn't destroy all that would be destroyed by breaking the engagement. Not least of which was his mother's hopes. She needed them now. He needed to keep his promise to her while he still could.

So instead he changed the subject. "Clarissa seems to be growing close to Li—to Mrs. Manning."

Kirkwood's eyebrow arched. "Yes. They seem to like each other, though there was no doubt it would be true. Mrs. Manning is a good friend of the Countesses of Delacourt and Ramsbury and Clarissa adores them. Mrs. Manning, on the other hand, does *not* seem to like you."

"Yes. Seemingly not," George admitted. "She told me as much at supper last night."

A choked laugh was the response. "So directly? Oh, I like her. Did she give any reason why?"

George paced off, flexing his hands at his sides. "My reputation. The fact I'm twelve years older than Miss Westinghouse. Lily was married to Thomas Manning somehow, can you believe it?"

There was a slight pause, but then Kirkwood said, "Old Manning?"

George nodded as he turned back. "Her sister has told me it was a happy marriage, but I wonder if it wasn't and that's influencing her feelings about me. I need to speak to her about it."

Kirkwood's lips pursed. "I see."

"What does that tone mean?"

"*Lily*"—Kirkwood accentuated her first name, leaving George to wonder if he'd slipped and used it, himself. He didn't think he had, despite the fact he only thought of her by her first name now—"is a beautiful woman."

"Fuck off." George glared at him, at his implication, even if it was perfectly true. Kirkwood implied he was attracted to her. He hated to admit that he was. It made him the exact bastard she believed him to be, didn't it? And somehow he wanted to prove her wrong. He didn't want her to see him as a villain, even if he feared he was.

Kirkwood rolled his eyes. "Fine, I'll change the subject. The chaos truly begins tomorrow, with the arrival of the close friends. Delacourt and Ramsbury will be here then. They're going to see through you, too."

"That's wonderful. You can all see whatever you all want, and gossip about it like a sewing circle if it makes you happy. But I said it once and I'll say it again: whatever you think you see or know, it changes *nothing*. I made a promise to marry Miss Westinghouse and I will. No one will stand in my way. Not you, not them, not Lily."

He pivoted to leave the room and it was only in the hallway that he realized he had *definitely* used her first name that time. And it only proved his friend's point further.

L ily was early when she came down for the drinks before supper that night and since she didn't wish to be the first one in the parlor, she entered the library instead. At least the books would be good companions. She didn't feel as though she was, herself. Her anxiety seemed to grow with every passing hour, even as she smiled and played cards with the women in the family and went on walks with her sister in the beautiful garden.

In the back of her mind, a constant refrain through it all, was *Lockhart, Lockhart, Lockhart.* Images of their night together would mix with her fears about her sister's future and it only resulted in nausea and worry.

She had taken two steps into the room when she came to a dead stop. As if she had conjured him with all her endless thoughts, Lockhart stood there at one of the tall bookcases, a novel dangling from his fingertips as he stared at her. She stared back and for what felt like forever, neither of them said anything.

The book clattered to the ground and the loud sound broke the spell. He muttered something beneath his breath as he bent to gather it back up and she swallowed hard before she spoke. "Forgive me, my lord, I didn't mean to intrude. I'll go."

She pivoted to do just that, but he lunged forward a long step and held out an hand as if to stop her. "Oh, please don't leave."

She stopped at the request and stared out at the escape of the hallway. Then she slowly turned to face him with what she hoped was a neutral expression. "Is there something you require, my lord?"

He shifted slightly, his discomfort as clear as her own. "You wanted to have a discussion with me last night at supper and I stopped it. But we're alone now, so it seems the best time to have it at last."

Lily worried her lower lip. She *had* wanted to put her fears about Alice's future into the open with him, but now it felt very dangerous to do so. Everything about this man felt dangerous. Yet she couldn't think of a way out of the situation, so she nodded. "Very well. Though if you think later would be better…"

"Tomorrow the friends will begin to arrive and then more and more guests afterward." For a brief moment, his expression grew troubled. "And then it will all be exhibition until the end."

"The end," she repeated. That didn't sound like a man happy to be marrying, it sounded like someone being marched to his doom. "You will be very busy, yes."

He smiled a little, though it didn't reach his eyes. "Well, my parents will be. I must just stand and smile."

"I see." She knew she sounded cold. In that moment she even managed to feel it at his description.

The smile fell from his lips and he ran his hand through his hair. She caught her breath, for when he mussed himself a little he looked even more like he had the night at the Donville Masquerade when he'd been all sin and reckless abandon.

"I suppose all that aligns with your concerns about me."

She forced her thoughts back to the moment and nodded. "I admit, it does. But I do want to apologize for being so forward at supper. To broach so tender a subject in a public forum was uncalled for. However, it doesn't change my fears."

He nodded slowly and then motioned to the chairs before the fire. "Will you sit with me and tell me more about those fears?"

She glanced at the comfortable chairs. They were turned toward each other and close together. Like they were meant for intimate reading with a friend or lover. It all felt too warm in that moment. Too close. But again, she had no choice here, so she took one seat and watched him fold his lanky body into the other. Their knees nearly touched and when he draped his arms over his thighs and leaned closer, fully focusing on her and whatever she would say, she almost couldn't breathe.

It was only thoughts of Alice that spurned her forward. "I-I hardly know where to begin."

He smiled again. "With my wicked reputation? Or perhaps the rumors of my layabout habits?"

Frustration rose in her chest, welcomed by her for it erased some of the other less appropriate feelings he engendered in her. "You tease about those things as if they won't affect my sister's future."

"I *do* take your sister's future seriously."

Another brief image of him rising above her, driving into her with all his passion came into her head and she snorted at the discordance of his words and what he'd been doing just a week before.

Suddenly he looked very serious, indeed. His gray-blue eyes darkened. "Do you have something to say to me, Mrs. Manning? Because that sound and the expression that goes along with it feels extremely personal."

"Alice is my sister. That makes *everything* personal to me."

"I meant personal *toward* me," he said, and leaned back. She could breathe a little more easily with the increased distance. "I know I've earned my reputation. Even if some of the stories are exaggerated, they come from a place of truth. And I'm—I'm not always proud of that."

She tilted her head. He sounded sincere when he said that. Almost torn. For a moment, she felt for him.

"*But—*" he continued, "I do intend to take care of my wife. To ensure she's as happy as she can be."

That should have soothed her but somehow it stung. She knew why and refused to acknowledge it or let inappropriate thoughts of this man enter her mind further as they talked.

"But what about other women?" she pressed.

His eyes widened. "I don't know what your marriage was like. Your sister implies it was a happy one."

She bent her head. It was so odd to discuss this with Lockhart when they'd had even more intimate discussions about her past that he didn't even recall. "Well, I've always protected my sister."

He was quiet a moment and his tone was gentler when he said, "I see. Men of our sphere, they often have mistresses. They often do not give much of a care about if their wives know their activities." There was something sour in his words, dark. "But I don't intend to do that."

"No?" She was surprised by that statement when she pondered what she knew of him, what she'd experienced with him, and the fact that she didn't think he'd ever even said Alice's name.

"I'd like to be better than how I was raised." His voice was rough and he gripped his hands against his thighs with those words.

She thought of how she'd watched the Earl and Countess of Pembrooke interact in the last two days. They were polite to each other, but there wasn't much warmth between them, even though Lady Pembrooke was very warm at her core. When she saw Lockhart with her, though, the two of them seemed close. He was always watching his mother, assisting her.

A few more pieces of the measure of this man fell into place and there was an intimacy to that. A connection like she'd felt when they lay in that bed together, when she'd felt comfortable enough with him to tell him a little of the story of her pain.

If he were being honest about these intentions he declared, she realized that meant the night in London had likely been a last night for him. A final excursion for the rake before he put on the moniker of decent husband. Did that make what had happened between them better or worse? She didn't even know anymore.

She swallowed. "Well, you seem the kind of man who could do anything he put his mind to."

He smiled once more and *there* was a flash of the rake in the expression, not dead in truth. And it made her toes curl in her slippers to see that. "I hope I can."

She leaned forward, but before they could continue the conversation, Alice came into the library. Both Lily and Lockhart turned toward her, getting to their feet. Guilt rushed through her at being caught this way, but Alice's face lit up with pleasure at finding them together.

"Oh, you are both here. Were you comparing books? Lily is a great reader, my lord."

He glanced at Lily one last time before he stepped toward Alice. "Are you, as well?" he asked.

Alice laughed and smiled at Lily over his shoulder. "Not nearly as much. I do enjoy some books, though. Not anything too serious, of course."

There was a flutter to his cheek and he inclined his head. "Well, you'll have plenty to choose from here at my parents' house and at my...at *our* homes in London or in the country. I am also a great reader." He glanced at the clock on the mantel. "But we will be late for the gathering. May I take you, Miss Westinghouse?"

Alice nodded and took the arm he offered. He began to lead her out, but at the door he cast his glance back at Lily. She could have told herself he was just making sure she was following, but their eyes met briefly and it wasn't just that. She could feel it. So she dropped her gaze and didn't let him see that what they'd talked about meant something to her.

That she wished things were different, but knew they never could be.

CHAPTER 9

George hadn't ever been one to focus endlessly on his troubles. Part of the joy of being a rake was that one was meant to play off anything serious. He'd always been good at doing just that, it was part of the mask he wore. But not now. Right now his problems and worries seemed to be turning into a wave and they threatened to wash over him and perhaps even drown him at last.

His intentions when he spoke to Lily in the library were to allay her worries, and in the process put an end to the confusion she created in him. But it hadn't worked. Instead, the spark of connection that had been borne when he told her things he normally kept to himself had only made him even more confused. And guilty. He felt guilty for a great many things.

For example, it was wrong to look at her across the parlor as he was now and mark every elegant movement of her hands as she spoke to his mother and Clarissa. To feel a stirring when she smiled or absently tucked a curl behind her ear. She was his future sister-in-law and he was feeling anything but brotherly.

Which only proved that her fears about him were founded in

reality. And that he was worse than the father he'd vowed to be better than.

"Lockhart?"

He started and glanced down to find Miss Westinghouse had joined him. She tracked his glance across the room and he shifted, hoping she wouldn't see his thoughts. It seemed she was oblivious, for she smiled.

"I'm so glad you and Lily are beginning to become friends," she said.

He almost laughed. He wasn't sure Lily wanted to be his friend any more than she had before she came into the library earlier in the night. *He* certainly didn't feel like her *friend*. No these sensations in his chest when she laughed softly were much more inappropriate than that.

"I realize it's important to you," he managed to croak out.

Her smile fell a fraction, but then she forced it back. "My mother wishes for me to play again tonight. You ought to dance with Lily. She's a wonderful dancer."

George closed his eyes for a beat. Dance with her. That meant touch her. Hold her closer than he could usually do in their positions in life. Perhaps it would be his only chance to do so. It was wrong, but he said, "If you would like me to, I'll ask her, of course."

"Oh yes, please."

Miss Westinghouse squeezed his arm awkwardly and then slipped off toward the piano. She sat and immediately her mother rushed to her side to turn pages. Lady Westinghouse looked around the room expectantly and loudly announced, "Alice will regale us with her talents again."

"I hope you'll all dance," Alice added, giving George a meaningful look.

There was no avoiding it now. He drew a breath and crossed the room toward Lily. His mother was already walking away and before George reached her, Kirkwood approached and said something to

Clarissa that made her blush before he guided her to the middle of the room so they could begin to dance.

That left Lily alone. Her eyes widened a fraction as he reached her and she dropped her gaze just as she always seemed to when he came near her. Like she was hiding from him. Why was she always hiding from him?

"Miss Westinghouse tells me you are a fine dancer, Mrs. Manning," he said softly. "And demands that I ask you to partner with me while she plays."

"Of course she does," Lily muttered under her breath. Then she gave a tight smile. "Well, if that is what Alice wants…"

He held out a hand and she stared at it a moment. He thought he heard her breath hitch a fraction, but then she caught his hand in hers. He ignored the frisson of awareness that raced through him and drew her to the center of the room.

The song Miss Westinghouse played was rather slow and to his horror, George realized the best dance for it was a waltz. It seemed Lily realized it in the same moment for her breath shuddered as she placed a hand on his shoulder and threaded her fingers through the opposite. She looked up at him and they began to move.

He stared down into her eyes and caught his breath. She was always so artfully dodging him, ducking away, that he hadn't gotten a good look at those eyes. They were brown, but it was so much more than that. They were bright, they almost sparkled. They put him to mind of…

He stumbled a little at the thought that filled his mind and had to correct himself so they didn't careen into Clarissa and Lockhart.

"Come now, Lockhart," Kirkwood teased. "Don't drag the poor woman hither and yon."

George managed a dim laugh, but he was still focused on Lily. Her eyes put him to mind of his Aphrodite from the Donville Masquerade the previous week. Her eyes had been just like that, hadn't they? Or was he misremembering? Was he just placing the image of one woman he wanted over another who he very much shouldn't as a form of self-torture?

She ducked her gaze slightly and he tightened his fingers against her hip. Her breath caught at that and she jerked that gaze back to his, only this time her pupils were dilated, her lips slightly parted, and in that moment he saw the truth.

Lily *was* the woman from the masquerade. There was no doubt about it anymore, it was as plain to him as his own name, as painful as his own mistakes. Those fascinating eyes widened and it was as if she could read him down to his very soul.

"Please," she whispered, swallowing hard.

That plea rocked through him, and now there was no doubt. How had he not recognized her from those eyes or her voice? Or *had* he down in some secret, dark part of himself and that was why he'd been drawn to this woman from the start even when she tried to dodge him at every turn?

"Lily," he said, his own tone low and harsh so the others wouldn't hear.

"No," she responded. "Please, please *don't.*"

"It was you?" he asked.

She didn't answer for a moment as they continued to turn, but her cheeks were bloodless now. Her hands shook in his. "I don't know what you mean." It was said so weakly.

His teeth clenched and he barely managed to speak from between them. "Don't lie to me."

Miss Westinghouse was finishing the song she was playing and the moment she did, Lily pulled from his arms.

"Oh no, Lily, keep going! I'm going to play a jig now," Alice called out, oblivious to the war going on between her sister and himself.

Lily gave a forced smile to her sister. "I would love to, but I find myself very tired. A slight headache. I should get some air. But please, do keep playing."

She gave George one last fleeting look and then she stepped from the room onto the terrace. He glared after her as the pieces of this puzzle continued to fit together. She had worn a mask, that was why he hadn't recognized her. But *he* hadn't. Which meant Lily had known who he was and what they had shared from the first time he entered the room a few days ago.

It explained everything: from her odd response to him from almost the first moment they 'met' to her intense worries about his future with her sister. She had *known* he was her Ares, her lover.

"I think I ought to go check on Mrs. Manning."

He jumped and turned to find his mother at his side. God, his mother. He was doing everything for her and if she ever discovered what had happened between him and his future wife's *sister*…

His stomach turned.

"Er, no," he said, squeezing her hand. "I-I'll go. Miss Westinghouse is determined the two of us should be friends and it will give me the opportunity to speak to her a moment."

His mother's brow wrinkled as she looked up into his face. "Are you well, dearest?"

"Perfectly," he lied, and turned away before she could see through him. Right now he feared he couldn't mask any of his roaring emotions.

He exited the room onto the terrace and shut the door behind him. Now that the eyes of the room weren't on him, he allowed himself a shaky breath.

"Fuck," he muttered.

Then he began to look around the dim terrace. He didn't see Lily immediately and pursed his lips. Had she run? Hustled over to one of the doors that led to another parlor and fled before there could be a confrontation? As if they could dodge this. Now that it was out there was nothing to do but face it. Hope it wouldn't destroy everything.

"Lily?" he called out in a harsh whisper.

There was no answer, at least not in words, but he heard a shuddering sob from a darkened corner of the terrace. He followed it and as his eyes adjusted, he saw her.

She was leaning on the stone wall of the terrace, her shoulders shaking. She turned to face him, and in the moonlight he saw her tears were bright on her face. Despite his confusion and upset at this untenable circumstance, he felt a powerful urge to comfort her. To wipe those tears away and somehow find a way to make this better.

"Please don't," she said. "Just go inside and we can pretend we don't know. That it never happened."

And there it was. The denials had been stripped away and the truth was laid bare. It was raw and powerful and changing. It was terrible and beautiful and wrong. Which meant the idea of doing what she suggested was ridiculous.

"Impossible," he snapped.

His breath was short as he recalled every heated moment of that night with her. Every soft shudder of her, every gasp and cry. He relived it all and wanted her just as powerfully now that he could see her entire face. Somehow he managed to push those feelings and desires away.

"Did you know who I was that night?" he asked.

Her lips parted and she stepped toward him, the color returning to her face but this time as heated anger. "How could you ask me that?"

"Because I don't understand one damned thing about this, nor about the fact that you said *nothing* to me when you must have known the truth immediately after your arrival. So I ask again, did you know that night?"

She shook her head. "Do you think if I had known that you were my sister's intended that I would have done those things with you? That I would have purposefully betrayed her in such a horrible way?"

He pursed his lips and some of his anger faded a fraction. "No. I've seen you with Miss Westinghouse. You care so deeply for her, I cannot believe you would do such a thing out of malice."

She reached back and steadied herself on the wall, another tear coming down her cheek. "But I did…I did do it."

"We did," he corrected her, and ran a hand through his hair as the full weight of this truth slammed down on his shoulders and threatened to crush him. "And yet you must have recognized me when you arrived, just as I already said."

"I-I did," she whispered, her voice breaking in the most heart wrenching way. "The moment you walked into the room that first day. I turned to look at you and my world collapsed around me like some house made of cards."

He stared at her, their eyes holding in the dim light. "Why didn't you say anything?"

She huffed out a breath and turned away, staring out at the garden. It took a moment for her to speak, but when she did she sounded steadier, like she was fighting to win back control. "You didn't recognize me thanks to the mask. I was the only one who knew, the only one caught in the web at that point. What should I have done, Lockhart? Taken you aside and told you that I was the woman you buried yourself in while you should have been preparing to wed my sister?"

"Yes, exactly that," he said. "Then we could have dealt with this together."

She pivoted. "How can it be dealt with? What we've done? Who we've betrayed? How can it *ever* be dealt with without destroying both our lives and the person I love most in this world?" Her voice broke once more and he flexed his hand at his side in a deep desire to touch her even though he shouldn't.

"Lily," he whispered.

She shook her head. "*No.* There is nothing to say or do, my lord. We must carry on just as we have been before the secret was fully revealed."

"How the hell can we do that?"

She drew a few deep breaths. "You've declared you will be a good husband to my sister. I choose to believe that because to imagine the alternative is too painful. And you and I will pretend that night never happened."

He stepped toward her and suddenly he could smell the intoxicating fragrance of her hair: citrus and gardenias. He wanted briefly to bury himself in that, in her and that was the material problem.

"Do you think that I could know this about you, that you were the woman that night, and not have it haunt me every time I look at you, Lily?" He moved even closer and all he wanted to do now was touch her face. "That I could be this near to you and not think of every touch? Every moan? Every grip of you?"

She was trembling as she stared up at him, but then she pushed her shoulders back and a steel came into her expression. "Well, you must. Because I'm not yours and you never should have been mine." She shoved past him. "You'll pretend it away just like I will."

"And what if I can't?" he asked, hating that it was true. That he feared it would always be true.

She looked at him over her shoulder once more. "Then I'll have to stay away," she said. "I'll have to see my sister without you being around. I'll have to separate myself. I would walk away rather than destroy her."

Her voice had elevated as she said those words and he opened his mouth to retort when the door to the terrace closed and they both turned to see who had intruded. It was Miss Westinghouse and she rushed toward them.

"Oh, please, you two mustn't argue," she said, her hands clasped before her. "I cannot bear it."

Lily's breath sucked in and out and she gave George a pleading look that all but broke his heart. She returned her gaze to her sister. "Dearest, what—what did you hear?"

"Just you speaking in a loud voice as I exited," Miss Westinghouse said, and glanced between them, her expression lined with worry. "And I can see your fraught expressions. It's obvious you two were arguing, that you have a strain between you, just as you seem to have had since Lily's arrival."

George ducked his head and fought to retain some control over his rolling emotions. He and Lily could not do this here, not now. She was right that they couldn't hurt Miss Westinghouse this way, even if he didn't think himself capable of just forgetting what had happened between them. That it wouldn't color the rest of his life the way that it had colored the last week since he'd touched this woman.

"We *were* having a disagreement," he said softly. "But you needn't worry."

"I must do," Miss Westinghouse insisted. She caught her sister's hand. "Lily, we must address the obvious, I think."

Lily paled further, if that was possible. For a moment he feared she would faint from lack of blood to the head. "The obvious?" she repeated.

"Yes. I *know* you have worries about this marriage because you don't always believe Mama has my best interest at heart. Because your own marriage was so happy that you only want the same thing for me."

Lily's lips tightened and she glanced again at George. Of course she would. He knew that secret, too. That her marriage had been anything but joyful.

"I don't want you to ever be unhappy," Lily said.

"Well, what makes me unhappy is that you two might not get along. That it would keep us separated as we have been these last six months. Being away from you has broken my heart and I cannot bear to think that could be the rest of my life." Miss Westinghouse's eyes filled with tears. "Whatever the troubles between you, won't you shake hands and agree to get along? Even if you cannot be friends at present, promise me that you won't be enemies. It's all I wish for."

She took Lily's hand, lifting it to her chest with a pleading look. Then, in what felt like slow motion, she extended it toward George. He realized she expected them to shake on it. For him to touch Lily and not react like she was the woman whose passion had set his world upside down.

Lily refused to look at him, but didn't draw her hand away. He extended his own and took it, letting his thumb slide across her skin before he shook it. Her breath hitched almost imperceptibly.

"My deepest apologies for my part in this, Mrs. Manning," he said.

Her lip trembled, but she schooled the reaction before she nodded. "And mine to you, Lord Lockhart."

"There," Alice said with a wide smile, as if all had been resolved. And for her, it had. "Now please come back into the parlor, won't you? Clarissa is playing the harp and it's so lovely."

She caught her sister's hand and together they walked back to the parlor doors. Lily glanced back at him over her shoulder, one last pleading look, and then she entered the room with her sister.

But even though this first confrontation was over, nothing had been resolved. And George had no idea what to do next when he was being pulled apart by what he had done, what he had promised, and what he wanted even though it was so very, very wrong.

CHAPTER 10

How Lily had made it through the rest of the previous evening, she didn't know. Somehow she'd talked to the others and smiled and pretended to listen to the music, all while the world was falling out from underneath her. She'd felt Lockhart's gaze on her far too often, his expression serious and dire.

She'd paced her room all night after, dressing gown flapping around her bare legs, reliving not only the moment when she'd realized he recognized her, but all those heated moments at the masquerade, only this time with the knowledge of who this man was, with the knowledge that he knew her too.

Now she stood in a parlor alone, still wracked by those memories and emotions. Only as time passed, as the shock and horror of his discovery of who she was faded a fraction, she felt something else: relief. It was a relief that she wasn't alone in this anymore. That she was no longer keeping the secret. It was theirs now.

Theirs. Nothing should ever be theirs. Not before. Not again.

She sighed and walked to the window to overlook the garden below. Servants were preparing a bowls field for ninepins, which seemed to be the next family activity for the day. She would have to stand close to Lockhart again, have to smile and pretend and know he was doing the same.

It wouldn't be the right moment to discuss the topic of their history, of course. But with more time between her and the revelation, she knew they must. They had to come to some accord for Alice, and for her own sanity.

How they could do that, she didn't know.

"Oh, Mrs. Manning, good morning again."

Lily turned toward the door with a smile as Lady Pembrooke entered the room. She was a striking woman, even at her advanced years. She had a gentleness to her, though. A kindness that seemed to permeate all interactions. Not to mention she looked very pretty in a fine blue-gray gown that matched her eyes, which Lockhart had inherited from her. Though when Lily looked closer, she noted that she looked a little tired.

"Good morning, my lady," she said. "That is a lovely gown."

"Thank you, my dear," the countess said, smoothing the lines of it with a blush. "I can give you the name of my seamstress if you like, she is a dream."

"That would be very kind," Lily said. She motioned to the window. "I see they're setting up for bowls. You did say at breakfast that there would be lawn games before luncheon."

"Oh yes." Lady Pembrooke joined her at the window. "Bowls are a favorite of both my son and my husband. We've spent many a fine afternoon playing over the years. Do you enjoy such games?"

"I do," Lily admitted. "There's nothing better than a rousing match in fine weather."

"Then you will do well with this family, for we're of a competitive mindset." The countess chuckled. "And what of your sister? Does Alice also like a hearty battle?"

Lily pursed her lips. Alice had never been one to be interested in observing sport, let alone participating in it. She was graceful as a dancer, but never on a field. "Alice is a bit…softer in her ways. She is more of an observer than player."

"Ah." Lady Pembrooke sighed. "Well, perhaps we can bring her out of her shell. George is very good at that sort of thing."

George. Lily hadn't dared to think of him by his first name since her arrival. Every little step toward further intimacy, even in her own mind, was so fraught with danger.

"I imagine he must be," she said softly. And she did. He was clearly the kind of man who brightened every room he entered. Who drew people to him like moths to his light. Certainly she had found him irresistible and now she would burn.

"Perhaps I'll pair you with my husband for the game, as I'm confident Kirkwood and Clarissa will wish to be together." Lady Pembrooke smiled. "Newlywed love, you know."

"They are very well matched. She seems vastly content with him."

Lady Pembrooke nodded. "She is. Our dear Clarissa had a difficult time of it, so to see her so very happy is wonderful. And he is an old friend to George, so we've known him since he was in short pants. Their marriage suits him, as well. I hope my son will ultimately be just as happy."

Lily cleared her throat, unwilling to get into a conversation about how Lockhart might be changed by marriage. "You said you would pair me with the earl. You don't intend to play, yourself?"

"No," Lady Pembrooke said after a little pause. "Not today, I think."

There was something in the lady's tone that made Lily look a little closer. Her gaze was clouded now, troubled. She stepped nearer to her hostess. "Are you—are you well, my lady?"

The countess's expression tightened a fraction. "Oh yes, my dear. You're very kind to ask. I'm just a bit tired, that's all. Now it looks as though the others are beginning to gather. Will you go down with me?"

"Of course," Lily said, though she remained a little troubled by the countess's behavior. It wasn't the first time she'd noticed the tension in the woman. Was she troubled by something regarding

Alice and Lockhart? Or was it something else that gave her that air of worry?

No, to wonder about that wasn't Lily's place. The woman wouldn't be *her* mother-in-law. She was nothing more than a kind stranger to Lily. She followed the countess from the room and together they made their way down to the garden. Indeed, the others were already gathered, talking and laughing together.

When Lily exited the house behind the countess, Lockhart's laughter faded, though. He held her stare a moment and then shifted his focus to his mother.

"And now we're all here," he said with a smile for her. "Let the battles begin. I intend to beat you this time, Mama."

The countess shook her head with a laugh. "I'm sure you would do so and so I won't even face off with you, so my record won't be risked. Mrs. Manning has kindly agreed to partner with your father so I may watch the festivities with Lady West-inghouse."

"Yes," Prudence said with a little glare for Lily. "I've never much liked lawn games."

"I see." Lockhart looked closely at his mother for a moment and then shifted to the rest with a wide smile. "Then let the best team win. And by that, I mean the team of Miss Westinghouse and me."

Alice tittered, but Lily could see it was with nervousness. They all took to the green and Lily gave the earl a little curtsey. "I hope I shall be a good partner to you, my lord."

He looked down at her with a smile that was so like his son's that she blinked in surprise. "Are you of a competitive nature, Mrs. Manning?"

She nodded, unable to do anything but return that dazzling smile. "I am, indeed, my lord."

"Excellent. Then I have no doubt we will *trounce them all.*" He said the last part with great emphasis, causing a laugh to rise up from all the others, including her sister.

And so for a little while, Lily pushed aside her troubles, and played a game that didn't involve hearts, just strategy. One she was far more certain she could win than the one that involved Lockhart.

~

George stood to the side of the lawn, watching as Lily and his father discussed tactics for their next roll. He hadn't been able to take his eyes off her all afternoon. She was very talented at the game, but she was also incapable of doing anything but charming everyone she met. His father was clearly taken with her, laughing at every little joke she made and cheering her on anytime she knocked down their pins.

It would be easy for her to fit into their group with her friendly, competitive nature. With her sister, it was a little more complicated. He glanced at Miss Westinghouse and found her staring off toward the house, her expression clouded. She was trying to match his play, her effort was undeniable, but she wasn't practiced at the game, it seemed. They were losing by a large number of points throughout the little tournament. Even more importantly, she seemed not to be enjoying the time they were spending together.

His father and Lily finished their turn and the next round of play was with Clarissa and Kirkwood. They appeared to be playing their own game. Though they were a team, they were equally competitive against each other, but there was a loving undertone to their interaction. Kirkwood couldn't stop smiling at his wife every time she knocked down the pins and spun on him with a triumphant cry of pleasure. So strange that not that long ago, his friend had been lamenting the circumstances that forced their union. And now...

Well, it was evident he had never been happier.

George looked again at Miss Westinghouse. "It will be our turn again soon."

She seemed a little startled by his statement, as if she had been leagues away in her mind. "Oh. Oh yes. I shall try to do better this round."

"You did fine the last few rounds," he tried to reassure her.

She laughed. "I may be naïve in a great many things, my lord, but I'm not a fool. I know I'm the worst player on the field. Nothing like my sister."

That last sentence hit him in the stomach like a punch, for it felt so true on so many levels. He pushed the inappropriate thought away and smiled at her. "Well, I'm certain you'll have much practice in the years to come, for this is a game we play with great gusto all summer long."

He hoped she would respond to that statement with something that would connect them, but she glanced at the ground instead. "Yes, so your mother said. I will try, of course."

She sounded so forlorn by the idea and for a moment he could see long years of his life stretching out, this woman barely tolerating or understanding his pursuits. She had already said she was no great reader, she didn't like lawn games, he had no idea of her thoughts on any topics that were his passions, actually. He didn't even know what any of hers were.

And yet he knew Lily far better. From her bad marriage to her love of books to the fact that she could hold her own on the field. Not to mention he knew her flavor and the sound of her shuddering breaths when she came.

Clarissa and Kirkwood finished their round and George motioned Miss Westinghouse to lead them to the lawn. She did so and took a deep breath while the servants reset the pins into their triangle shape. When she bowled, the ball rolled to the side and she only knocked down two pins.

She glanced at him. "I really am rubbish at this. You'll have a challenge in your roll."

He shook his head to reassure her even though she wasn't wrong and they finished the round still far behind the others. That concluded the game and made his father and Lily the winners. The earl crowed, shaking her hand with enthusiasm as she laughed.

"Good show, my dear, good show," he said, and then started

toward George's mother. "If you are resting yourself, you may always pair me with this young lady, Louisa. She is a fine player."

"I shall keep it in mind," his mother said with a laugh.

Miss Westinghouse gave George an apologetic look and then returned to her mother and his parents. Clarissa and Kirkwood were to the side of the lawn, deep in what seemed to be intimate conversation as he pushed a lock of hair off her cheek.

George sighed but then straightened as he noticed Lily was approaching him. She appeared...*determined*. And beautiful with her wind-tousled hair. Why did she have to be so beautiful, no matter her mood? That seemed incredibly unfair.

She stopped beside him and together they looked off at the others.

"Good game, Mrs. Manning," he said.

She glanced up at him at last. "Your father is excellent. I merely felt compelled to match him."

"A great many have tried and never done as well," he said. "I also believe you've wrapped him around your little finger, so well done."

She let out her breath. "I think you and I must discuss our...our situation."

He turned toward her. "Yes. Last night we were both at high emotion. It was not a productive conversation. But obviously we must work this out and discuss it rationally."

"If that is even possible. The situation itself seems to lack rationality." She shook her head. "We must also be somewhere that won't allow interruption. My sister could have overheard us on the terrace and that would have been a further disaster."

He glanced off, trying to think of someplace where they might be alone but wasn't a dangerous option. He saw the tower from the old castle in the distance and said, "What about the tower?"

She looked toward it and he thought he saw a little pleasure on her face when she found it. "Oh, I have wondered about that place. Before I saw you, realized who you were, it was even suggested you would be my guide in exploring the old castle site."

"Then it won't seem odd if I offer. Why don't you say something about it now while the others are preparing to go inside, and I'll gallantly offer to guide you?"

"Won't others want to come along?" she asked.

He laughed despite the fraught situation. "I promise you, I'm the only one who has any interest in the tower. I've bored them all to tears with my obsession with it over the years. They'll likely be happy I have a new victim to torture with my tour."

"Very well," she said, and then took a big breath like she was gearing herself up for this. "Is that the tower from the old castle site in the distance, my lord?" she asked in a louder voice so the others would hear.

"Oh no," Clarissa said with a teasing groan as she and Kirkwood rejoined the group. "Don't get my cousin started on his tower, he'll never let you escape it!"

George stuck his tongue out at her and she returned the look playfully. "They're just jealous that they don't have a castle of their own."

"You *don't* have a castle of your own," Kirkwood snorted. "You have half a crumbling tower."

"You said you wished to have a tour of it, I think, Mrs. Manning, when you arrived," Lady Pembrooke said with a shake of her head at the others. "George, you could take her. Perhaps Alice could join you."

As both George and Lily froze, Alice glanced back at them and then up at the house. "Oh, I've had the tour," she said slowly. "As much as I enjoyed it, I think all this excitement has worn me out. You go, Lily. I think you like that sort of thing a great deal more than I do." She gasped as she realized how that sounded and color filled her cheeks. "Not that I didn't enjoy every moment of your tour, my lord."

Kirkwood laughed. "Oh dear, you have already driven this poor girl to the edge of boredom, Lockhart. Badly done."

"Well, if Mrs. Manning is a more intelligent person than the rest of you." He halted and smiled apologetically at his fiancée. "Except for Miss Westinghouse, of course, I'm happy to take *her* for a tour." George looked at her. "We could go now while the rest of them take their rest."

"Yes, that would be fine," Lily said, and the relief was plain on her face. They had made their arrangements. They would get their time alone to discuss all that needed to be discussed.

And George could only hope that all the things he actually wished to do to this woman when they were alone would fade in the background when they were finally away from the others. Because he couldn't want her.

CHAPTER 11

As the others returned to the house, Lily and Lockhart remained on the bowling field, watching them go. Alice was at the rear of the group, and she kept looking up at the house. Lily noted that she never once looked back at them, never sought Lockhart's gaze. Funny, because all Lily wished to do was find it. Hold it. Lose herself in it. No matter how dangerous and wrong that desire was.

She drew a shaky breath and turned toward him. "Shall we go, my lord?"

He nodded and for a moment she thought he might offer his arm. His elbow tipped toward her a fraction and the world slowed. But then he shook his head, his cheeks brightening with color and motioned toward their destination.

"Of course." Together they began the walk down toward the tower and he glanced at her from the corner of his eye. "Are you truly interested in the history of the place? Or is it only a good excuse?"

"Oh, no I'm very much interested," she admitted. "I love to explore the history of old manor estates."

He seemed to brighten a little at that answer. "Well, then perhaps I can tell you a bit."

"Yes, please. At the very least it will be a pleasure before... before..."

He nodded as if he understood. "Yes. Well, the family has held the title since the 1400s. The castle was a fortification, especially during the Hundred Years War. Henry V even stayed here a while."

"That's very exciting," she said, and meant it. The idea of having a home where the famous king had stayed was a thrill. "How did it come to be replaced by the current home?"

Lockhart rolled his eyes. "You know how those with power and money are. They sometimes don't take care of their responsibilities. The castle was left in disrepair while the family stayed in other places. It began to rot. About seventy years ago, my great-great grandfather decided he wanted a fine new manor house and began dismantling it to have Pembrooke Hills built as it is now. Much of the old stone and timber was used in the construction, but the tower remains."

"I noted the tapestries in some of the parlors," she said. "Was the one with the lions depicting Henry from back then? Some of the hills around him look like those here."

He came to a stop and stared at her. "Yes," he said. "Great God, Lily, I don't think anyone else has ever noticed that. Indeed, those were made after one of his stays here to celebrate the honor."

She couldn't help but smile in pride at his astonishment. He seemed truly pleased that she cared about this topic and she couldn't deny that she liked pleasing him. Too much. Luckily her thoughts were drawn away from that fact because they were almost at the tower now and it rose up in all its tarnished glory. There were remnants of broken walls near it, overgrown with grass, shrubs and flowers that poked their heads out from between gaps in the stones.

"It's lovely," she breathed, and stepped forward. "Oh, it must have been *magnificent* in its prime."

"Yes," he said, wistfulness to his tone. "I wish I could have seen it as it was. I can imagine it, of course, and spent many a day as a boy doing just that. I fought a great many battles defending the old castle, I admit."

She laughed. "Oh, that's a very sweet thought."

"Sweet?" he scoffed. "No. Never. Well, perhaps. A child doesn't understand war, so I think it was all a bit romantic to me." Their eyes locked a moment and he cleared his throat before he continued, "There are old plans in the library, some sketches here and there and a few paintings. I can show you them later if you'd like. But when you stand here where she used to be, you feel how wonderful she was." He sighed. "Perhaps when I'm earl, I'll do a little renovation. At least bring the tower back to her former glory."

She faced him and found him staring up at the remains, his expression far away. The sunlight was on his face and he looked so...different. Not just the confident rake who could seduce with the cock of an eyebrow, but something deeper. More interesting, at least to her.

"I think that's a wonderful idea," she said softly.

He glanced at her and for a moment their eyes held. Then he looked away. "Would you like to look inside?"

"Oh yes!" she said, and followed him as he led her carefully over the broken stones and knotty bushes that grew up in the open spaces. "What were the men doing that first day when I arrived? The ones you helped with the horse."

"Oh," he said. "When areas of the new house and stables need masonry repair, they come and collect stones here."

"That makes perfect sense, they're the perfect match after all." She drew in a breath as he unlatched the tower door and pushed it open with a creak.

She stepped in and drew in a deep breath of the cold, wet smell of the stone. It was dim inside, the only light coming from the small, uncovered windows high above. The space where they stood was large and open. There was a trap door on the floor and then a small opening that led to spiraling stairs.

"I'd take you up, but it's narrow and not very safe," he said. "The trap door leads to what was once the castle prison."

She looked at him with a laugh. "You have your own prison? I'll try not to break any rules, then." He swallowed and she realized how those teasing words could sound. She smoothed her hands over her skirt and then said, "It's wonderful. I can see why you're fascinated. And I can think of five different things you could do with this tower if you do decide to recover it to its full beauty over time. Thank you for showing me."

"Of course."

He stepped back out of the door and she followed. Once more they picked their way through the stones. They were almost past the outer walls of the original structure when her foot caught on a hidden root of a bush and she staggered. As much as she tried to right her balance, she couldn't. He seemed to realize it, for he grabbed for her hand as she stumbled forward and she hit his chest with her full weight. His arms came around her to steady her and for a moment all time stilled.

She stared up at him, trying not to react to the clench of his fingers against her spine, the warmth of his chest against hers. His breath was short and his pupils dilated. There was no doubt that he, like her, was moved by this. That he recalled just as easily the last time they'd been in each other's arms. And how effortlessly they could go back to that moment, forget themselves and surrender to the desire that still pulsed here, dangerous and wrong.

It took all her self-control to extract herself from his embrace and step back. She dropped her gaze from his and sighed. "If we cannot find a way to…to fix this, I'll have to leave. To protect her, to keep from ruining her future, I'll have no choice."

He let out a low sound that was almost pained. "I know. But *how* do we fix it? It happened. And there are echoes of it everywhere just like the echoes of our voices bouncing off the rocks in that big tower."

Tears stung at that statement, but she blinked them back. "I feel them too. The memories of that night just…sit in my head. Before I knew the truth, I liked having them there. Liked reliving that stolen night with a man whose face I'd likely never see again."

"Until you did," he said softly.

She nodded. "Now when those memories come back it's not just some wicked gentleman who played my desire until it sang. It's *you*, Lockhart."

"I'm sorry," he said. She could tell he meant it.

"It's not your fault," she said. "We didn't know. You were in the hell looking for a last night before your future was set. Wasn't that it?"

He nodded slowly. "Yes, exactly that. I was putting away the past."

"And I-I don't know what I wanted."

His gaze snagged hers again. "No?"

There was too much heat between them again. Too much weight in that one little word that challenged her and made her body react in ways it most definitely shouldn't.

She ducked her head. "You gave me what I wanted, Lockhart. George. I don't…" She knew she shouldn't say these words, but somehow she needed to. "I don't regret it, despite it all."

"Neither do I." His voice was rough, filled with heat.

She turned away and paced the grass a moment before she faced him again. "Can we just pretend like we were different people? Like we were just those strangers after all, who reached for each other in that dreamy place? Can Aphrodite and Ares exist outside of Lily and Lockhart so that we don't destroy everything in the real world?"

There was a long hesitation and then Lockhart bent his head. "We can try, Lily."

There was something about the way he said *try*. Just a little emphasis that made her doubt it was possible. But she had to cling to it anyway, because if she didn't then she'd lose too much. It would tear her from her sister or at least mar the closeness she wanted to reform once Alice was no longer under the thumb of Lily's stepmother.

But she'd also lose all access to this man. She'd have to force herself away from him and teach herself to hate the night they'd shared so it wouldn't burn a hole through her. She didn't want to do that. She wanted to keep it as a pretty little secret she could draw out and recall for her own pleasure. Something sacred, not sullied.

"The others arrive tomorrow," he said, motioning toward the house. "Having more guests here will help us create space between ourselves."

"I've thought the same thing. You'll have even more duties to fulfill, as will I, so it will make sense that we won't be in each other's paths all the time."

"We'll separate to our respective friends and family members, we'll keep our contact at a minimum except when it cannot be avoided without causing questions." She must have revealed a little of her feelings on her face because he took a long step toward her. Too close and yet still too far. His breath was ragged as he added, "And we'll keep whatever we think of that, of each other, a secret."

She nodded, for every word made sense, even if she wasn't certain they could keep those promises. Not when the moment they were near each other, everything became raw. "That—that's for the best."

He stared at her a long moment. "What I would do to kiss you right now. For the last time."

"If you kissed me, I think it would make it worse," she whispered, even though she ached for him to do just that. "And it would be wrong. Before we didn't know, now we do." She held out a hand. "Goodbye, Ares."

He took her hand and held it, cupping it between his, stroking his fingers over hers gently. Then he lifted it to his lips and kissed her knuckles. "Goodbye, my Aphrodite."

She turned away from him, bringing her trembling hand to her chest where she clutched it to her pounding heart. Then she took a deep breath and forced herself to become Mrs. Manning again. Sister of the bride. Nothing more to this man than a future family member.

"So, Lord Lockhart," she said. "Does your own estate have any ruins or kingly visits to brag about?"

He was quiet a moment and his voice was rough as he joined her for the walk back to the main house. He put his hands behind his back as they strolled casually. "No. The seat of the viscounty is, sadly, entirely boring. Though it has a nice lake for fishing and beautiful hills to ride through. Does your sister…does *Alice* like that sort of thing?"

She glanced at him. "Well, the riding, yes."

"Well, there you have it. Something in common," he said with a smile that didn't reach his eyes. "I'll have to tell her all about our fine horses. She'll have whichever one she wishes as a wedding gift from me."

Lily nodded and they were silent the rest of the way to the house. But the pain she wished she could erase was still there. And she could only hope that it would fade to nothingness at some point.

～

Although George had lived a life packed with excess, one place where he'd never delved too deep was with drink. He liked his port and his whisky and his wine, but he rarely got deep in his cups. Tonight, standing on the terrace after the day's events, staring up into the starry night, he wanted nothing more than to get blind drunk. It would numb the pain in his chest, at least, the one that hadn't faded since he'd parted ways with Lily earlier in the afternoon.

What they had agreed upon was *right*, of course. But it still burned. All of this still burned.

"George?"

He turned to find Clarissa coming out onto the terrace. She shut the door behind herself, tightened her wrap around her shoulders and stepped up to join him. He smiled and there was at least some pleasure that was real in the expression. He'd always adored his cousin, even if they'd been so very opposite. Clarissa had grown up obsessed with propriety thanks to the cruel expectations of her parents, while he had taken a road of dissipation.

To see her content now, loved, accepted, and by one of his own best friends? Well, that was at least something of joy in the darkness that currently surrounded him.

"Happiness becomes you, Clarissa," he said, and sipped the drink he'd brought out to nurse in the starlight. "And no one deserves it more."

She smiled at him. "Well, perhaps you do," she said.

He snorted his derision. "What have I ever done to deserve happiness?"

She seemed surprised at the sharpness of his tone. "George, you have always been kind to those who needed it, including myself."

"Hmmm. Well, that is because only a fool wouldn't be kind to you."

She was quiet and looked up at the stars with him. "What are you looking for out here all alone?" she asked.

He flinched. He could have lied, but he was too tired. "Mars," he said. "The planet of war."

She looked up at him and from the corner of his eye he could see the confusion and concern mixed on her face. "Well," she said slowly, "I believe it is that one with the reddish tint, right there."

He followed where she pointed and found the little ruddy star that was so far away. It made sense that it was red. Like blood.

"Why are you looking for that?" she asked. "I don't recall you ever being that interested in astronomy."

He took another sip of his alcohol and welcomed the burn and the increasing muddiness it created. "Ares and Aphrodite."

She wrinkled her brow. "You're thinking of Greek mythology?

Careful, cousin, tread too far into history and antiquities and you'll lose your card as a rake."

"I'm surrendering it anyway," he muttered. She was quiet a moment and he stared up for a bit longer, his mind rolling over pains and thoughts. "Did you know that Ares and Aphrodite were separated after their affair? That they were forced to love each other from afar forever?"

"I suppose that happens in many of the myths. Affairs lead to consequences and often new affairs." Clarissa didn't seem to notice when he flinched. She added, "Anyway, they weren't *entirely* separated. I think I recall that they often made their way to each other in secret."

He almost laughed, or perhaps it was cried. Hard to separate the two in that moment. "Lucky them."

He was revealing too much in his slightly tipsy state. That was proven when Clarissa turned toward him and took his hand. "George, is…is Alice a good match?"

He jerked his gaze down toward her. "There's nothing about the young lady that doesn't recommend her."

"That's true." Clarissa shook her head. "She's so kind and sweet-natured. She's certainly beautiful. But that isn't what I meant. Is she a good fit for *you*?"

He didn't answer for long enough that the question began to answer itself and they both knew it. He shrugged at last. "She's my fiancée."

Clarissa sighed softly. "I see. Forgive my disappointment, I had only hoped you might find—find love."

He flinched again. Love. He'd never believed in it. He'd scoffed at it. Now the idea of it stung. "That was your fairytale, not mine, cousin. It would be repetitive to have the same story played out in one family."

He meant it to tease, but he could see she didn't find it amusing.

"But—" she began.

He faced her. "I'm going to do the unexpected, you know."

"What's that?"

"Keep my promises. Be a better man."

They both knew what he meant. She'd been around his father and mother long enough to see the cracks in their union. To know why they were there.

She touched his hand. "But you *are* a good man, George. What-ever wrongs you think you must atone for, yours or…or someone else's, you deserve to be happy."

He wasn't certain of that anymore. He wasn't certain of anything. "Come, I'll take you inside. I'm sure your husband must be waiting on you to go upstairs together. You shouldn't waste your time trying to comfort a rake who is brooding like a gothic hero."

She clearly wished to argue, but there must have been something to his expression that stopped her. She only sighed and allowed him to take her in.

He could only wish her words didn't echo the rolling feelings in his tight chest. He could only wish he didn't want those same things for himself.

Things that were most definitely out of reach. Unlike the bottle he intended to take to his bed so he'd forget them.

CHAPTER 12

Lily stood on the portico of the manor house the next morning, watching as a carriage rolled up the drive. Under normal circumstances, she would have been thrilled to welcome the arrival of her friends to the party. Especially since she and Lockhart had agreed to use the additional guests to create distance between them.

But as she watched Esme exit the carriage, balancing on her husband's hand before she rested a palm on her pregnant stomach, Lily could only feel fear. Her friend was too observant not to see there was something wrong. She would ask questions. When she found out the answers, because she *would* find them out, her feelings for Lily would have to change. How could they not after what Lily had done?

Still, she forced a smile as Esme's sister-in-law and brother-in-law joined the Delacourts on the drive. The Earl and Countess of Ramsbury were as in love as Esme and Finn. And just as kind and accepting people.

Right now all of that felt stifling.

She watched as the group greeted the others, shaking hands and exchanging hugs and everyone was talking at once. Marianne and

Esme were already close to Clarissa and had welcomed her into their circle after her marriage. They were immediately just as friendly toward Alice, drawing her in and making her sister's cheeks bright with their compliments. It was clear it put Alice at ease, for which Lily adored them. They'd be a fine circle of friends, and she would be…well, she'd be on the outside, wouldn't she? Even though she'd be included, she wouldn't have what they had. And she would always be sharply reminded of what she'd done and lost when she was with them all.

She shook away those maudlin thoughts as best she could and tried to keep the smile on her face. Soon, Esme's gaze fell on her and her friend broke from the chatting crowd and came to her. Esme wrapped her arms around her and gave her the tightest hug she could with her child separating them.

"You look beautiful," Lily managed to squeak out. "Glowing."

Esme leaned back and her sharp gaze rolled over Lily in one sweep. "And you look…what is wrong?"

"Oh, damn you," Lily said, almost laughing when what she really wished to do was have a good, hard cry. "Don't start with that."

Esme didn't smile, but wrinkled her brow. "What is it?" she asked again, dropping her voice even lower so no one would overhear.

Lily shut her eyes briefly and immediately Esme caught her arm and called to the others. "My dearest Lily and I are going to take a walk in the garden so I might stretch my legs. We'll join you all for tea shortly." She hauled her off without awaiting a response. Once they'd moved away a few steps, Esme leaned in closer and whispered, "Now, what is the best way to get to the garden?"

Lily didn't argue or fight her, just drew her around the back of the house and into the garden behind it. They moved onto the paths and Esme's grip tightened on her arm.

"Obviously something has happened," Esme said. "I can see it all over your face. I'm certain you've had no one to talk to about whatever it is since your arrival. I know you too well to think you'd trouble your sister when she's so close to her wedding and God knows that wicked stepmother of yours is no support. So tell me."

Lily managed to detach herself from her friend and moved to a bench in the middle of the garden. With a sigh, she sat down and rubbed a hand over her face. What Esme offered was the most torturous temptation. She wanted and feared it in equal measure.

"Lily!" Esme's tone was sharper now, laced with fear not just concern.

"If I tell you," Lily finally gasped out, "you'll surely despise me for what I've done."

Esme's eyes went wide at that suggestion. She approached more carefully now, as if she saw Lily as a wounded animal who needed to be treated with care. Funny, for that was just how she felt.

She joined Lily on the bench and turned a little to fully face her. "When I was gone, missing all those years, I spent some time as a lightskirt in parts of London you've probably never visited, nor even heard of," she said without preamble. "And when I couldn't bear that anymore, I became a popular female pugilist. And then I met Finn at the Donville Masquerade and he pulled away all my masks. Literally and figuratively. Which is how I ended up head over heels in love and back home."

Lily stared at her in stunned silence, mouth dropped open in the most unladylike fashion thanks to the shock of what she'd just heard. There had been a great deal of speculation about her friend's whereabouts during a long absence from Society. Lily had feared for Esme's safety during that dark time, even sometimes wondered if she were still alive. When her friend returned, even when she'd insisted on being called Esme, a shortened version of her middle name rather than Charlotte, which was what she'd been known as her entire life before, Lily hadn't pushed. She hadn't wanted to cause any pain or make things worse, especially when Esme was so happy with her life at present.

But now her friend spilled it all out, chin lifted and shoulders straight.

"I cannot believe it," Lily breathed at last. "Oh, Esme, how awful."

"Some of it was," Esme said with a little shrug. "And much of it wasn't. It changed me, it scarred me…but it also shaped me into what I am today and brought me to this life. So I wouldn't change a thing, good or bad. Now that you know the truth, the secrets I've kept from you, do *you* despise *me*?"

She asked the question with great confidence, but Lily saw a little flash of fear in Esme. She was offering vulnerability and it wasn't given lightly. Lily took her friend's hand. "I could *never.*"

Esme's expression softened. "Then please trust that I could also *never* despise you for anything you've done. It can't be more shocking than what I just told you."

Lily bent her head. "And yet you might be wrong."

Esme's concern returned. "Great God, Lily, you're truly starting to frighten me. Please tell me."

Lily let out her breath, dropped her voice and then told Esme everything. She told her about her night at the Donville Masquerade and the man who had made every wicked dream she'd never dared acknowledge come true. And she told her what had happened when she realized that same man was the very one marrying her sister.

She let it all fall away, fighting tears with every word and finally let out a shaky sigh when she finished. Esme was staring at her with much the same shocked expression as Lily had felt on her own face just a moment before. At last Esme shook her head.

"Well. I'll be damned."

"No, I think that's me," Lily said. And then to her horror, she began to cry.

Esme wrapped an arm around her shoulders and for a little while she just held her like that, silently comforting and allowing Lily to finally fully pour out all the emotion she'd been trying to keep inside in order to protect her sister and herself. Once she could collect herself, it *did* feel better to have finally released it all. To have someone other than Lockhart who knew the truth. Someone who was only on her side about it.

Esme wiped some of the tears from Lily's face gently and then she asked the question Lily had been trying to avoid in herself since her arrival. "Are you in love with Lockhart?"

Love. That word should have been soft and gentle and kind. It wasn't. It was hot and harsh and painful in every nerve ending, in every vein. She bent her head and whispered, "I am...I'm falling in love with him, I fear. Yes."

Esme's little *oh* ricocheted through her. "I'm so sorry, dearest. And does he also have feelings for you?"

She looked up toward the house. Somewhere up there, Lockhart was having tea and smiling politely and she also knew, like she knew her own hand, that he was wondering where she was. Wondering if she was well.

"We were both shaken by the power of what happened at the Donville Masquerade," she said. "That night we talked about it, as we lay together, er...*after.* There was no denying the connection from the moment we met, the second we touched. He made me feel so safe. So alive. And not just because he bedded me. And later... later after he discovered the truth, we talked again. We couldn't deny that night meant something to both of us."

Her breath was short now. Harsher. She stopped talking and shifted in the seat, trying to find some modicum of calm and decorum. There was none left. She whispered, "If he—if he were free—"

She broke off. She couldn't finish that sentence. It would be further opening a Pandora's box of her heart when the demons were already flying out of it. When her world was already being torn apart by them.

There was a long pause, and Esme didn't break her gaze from Lily's face for a moment of it. Finally, she said, "Is there no way around it? No way that he *could* be free?"

"Not without breaking my sister. Alice doesn't love him, I know it, I can see it. But to have the engagement broken so close to the marriage? To have it be *me* who caused that? I'm sure it would hurt her, both materially on the marriage mart and also down to her soul."

"And you love her almost as your own."

"She practically was. Prudence is no mother to her. Or at least she wasn't until Alice reached the age my stepmother could use her for her benefit." Lily sighed. "She's kept me away from her almost all of the last six months."

"Why?" Esme asked. "I've never understood that, but I didn't want to pry and make things worse."

"Since I arrived and have seen the situation for myself? I think she did it to keep me from intervening on my sister's behalf," Lily said. "From questioning the prudence of the match before the contracts were signed and the announcements made." She hesitated and shook her head. "And likely Prudence did it for her own cruel entertainment. She's has always despised me."

"Because she's a wretched cow who deserves a right cross," Esme muttered. When Lily's eyes widened, she shrugged. "I don't punch people anymore. Something about it not being very countess-y. I'd be willing to break that rule for you, but I think you'd say no."

Lily smiled at the joke, or at least she *thought* it was a joke. It felt so good to be able to do so after how fraught this conversation had been. "It's tempting, but better not, it would only lead to even more trouble for all of us. At any rate, whatever Prudence's reasons, the fact is I've felt the sting of that separation. And if I did this to Alice, if Lockhart and I moved forward with this thing between us, I'm certain I'd be parted from my sister again. Probably permanently. I couldn't bear it."

There was no playful teasing in Esme anymore when she took Lily's hand gently. "So what will you do?"

Lily swallowed past the lump in her throat. The one that hadn't really gone away, that she feared would always be there, a reminder that devastation was also right there. That loss would be permanent the moment Lockhart stared into her sister's eyes and pledged his life to hers.

"I'll pretend," she whispered. "And I'll do my best to separate myself from him and from this. For both our sakes."

Esme squeezed the hand she held gently. "I hate this. I want to see you have the love you deserve. It breaks my heart that you're going through this. *But* if this is what you feel must happen, I'm here now. I'll do everything I can to help you."

"But you…you won't say anything to anyone, will you?" Lily asked, glancing again at the house. "Delacourt is such good friends to Lockhart, and the men are all so close to each other. I wouldn't want them all to know what I said, what I did."

Esme's brow wrinkled. "It isn't my secret to tell. I wouldn't reveal your confidence. Not to my husband, not to anyone else."

"Thank you," Lily said, and then sighed as she got up. "And now we must join the others. And you can watch me pretend."

"I've had a lot of practice pretending," Esme said as she took her arm and they walked together back to the house. "I could even give you advice on it."

"I'll take all I can get, and all the support you're so kindly offering," Lily said as they headed up the stairs. Back to the others, back to the countdown to the moment all this would be irrevocable.

Now that the closest friends had joined the party, George and his parents hosted the first ball of the wedding gathering. Because the lion's share of the important guests who would arrive in the next week for the final days before the service weren't there yet, they had invited in their tenants and local gentry. It was a way to celebrate with those in Pembrooke Hills, to specially include them in the joy.

A wonderful sentiment, and yet George felt very little joy as he stood to the side of the dancefloor, watching Lily as she took a turn with Sir William Walters, their kindly neighbor just one estate over.

The older man was clearly taken by her, laughing at something she said as they danced a lively jig. Of course, that bright wonder had been the reaction of every single person she had interacted with all night. She had such an easy way of drawing people to her, giving them the remarkable gift of her full attention, putting them at ease with a smile or a laugh or a gentle touch.

The song ended and she left the dancefloor with Sir William, the pair returning back to his wife. Lily spoke to them for a moment, smiling and nodding at everything that was said. When she slipped away from them, they exchanged a smile, spoke together a moment. George's chest ached and a horrible, prodding thought entered his mind:

She would have made the perfect viscountess. And later the most wonderful countess.

He pursed his lips and forced himself to look for Miss Westinghouse. No, Alice. He was trying very hard to begin thinking about her as Alice. Referring to her as Alice.

She was standing with a few of the tenants. Like her sister, she seemed fully engaged with them but there was little of the warmth and connection there. Not that it was her fault. She hadn't much experience with such things. Alice was very young.

That fact gave him no pleasure. They had so little in common.

"Fuck," he muttered, and crossed to the terrace doors to get some air. He would take a break, he would refocus just as he and Lily had sworn they would continue to do. Eventually this...this infatuation with her would pass. He would make it be so.

He exited onto the broad, stone terrace that wrapped around a good portion of the back of the house. Drawing in a deep breath of the cool night air, he walked around to a shadowy corner where he might have a moment's privacy even if someone else came outside.

He leaned on the stone edge of the terrace wall and looked out at the garden. A few ornamental lamps had been lit so that the pathways were visible to guests and as his eyes adjusted to the darkness, he saw that just below the terrace, right at the entrance to the garden, Lily was now standing beside one of those lamps. She must have slipped from the ballroom while he was distracted. She wasn't alone. Her stepmother stood with her and the two women seemed to be involved in an intense conversation.

He strained to hear, but the air didn't carry the words up to him. He was going to turn away, stop involving himself in Lily's life, when suddenly Lady Westinghouse stepped up to her, extended a finger and poked Lily's chest hard.

"If...ruin...pay." The harsh, broken sound of the words carried, and though he didn't know exactly what had been said, the intent was clear.

Lily said something soft back to her and Lady Westinghouse pivoted away and stormed to the stairs. She rushed past George's hiding place without even noticing him there and hustled back into the ball.

When he looked down at Lily again, she stomped one foot a few times and let out a gasping cry of frustration and anger that was clearly not meant for anyone else to hear. Once again, he knew what he should do. He should go back inside, dance with his fiancée, forget he'd spied on something that was none of his affair.

And once again, he did the opposite because he couldn't seem to resist this woman. He made his way to the stairs and came down into the garden.

"Lily?" he called out softly.

She had her back to him and she pivoted toward him, eyes wide and voice shaking when she said, "Lockhart?"

"Yes." He stepped closer, watching how her hands fluttered at her sides when he did. Watching how her pupils dilated ever so slightly when he came close enough to observe every twitch of her mouth and sound of her breath. "Are you well?"

"Of course. Why would I not be?" Her voice broke a little and she folded her arms like a shield before her.

He didn't believe her, he wouldn't have even if he hadn't spied on her a moment before. He realized she had a sound to her voice when she was strained. A little lilt that was almost imperceptible and yet he perceived it. Even if he shouldn't.

"I saw you with your stepmother," he said. "The interaction seemed unpleasant."

At that, her shoulders loosened and rolled forward and she looked up at the stars with a long, exhausted sigh. "Damn. Well, I'm embarrassed you'd see such an exchange. Did you hear it, as well?"

He shook his head. "Just a few broken words. It was obvious she was angry with you. I know your relationship is fraught, but what is it that upsets her so much?"

Lily looked at him a long moment and he could see her fighting whether or not she should offer him such an intimate glimpse into her life. They both knew the answer, and yet she didn't seem to be able to fight this pull any more than he did. Was that good or bad?

She walked toward the fountain a few feet from the lamp where they'd been standing and watched for a moment while the little marble cupid poured water from a jug into the larger fountain base. "I was only ten when my mother died. It was so sudden and so awful."

"How?" he asked gently. He shifted because the idea of the loss of a mother was very sharp to him at present. But to lose her as a child…that was heartbreaking.

She glanced at him. "She caught a fever and she faded so quickly. I was very close to her, I adored her and it broke my heart. My father hardly waited out the expected mourning period before he remarried. Prudence was only ten years my senior and I realize now she was already pregnant with Alice when they married."

"That must have hurt you."

"It was very confusing in the midst of all my grief. And she didn't make it easier. She wanted her viscount, her title, but she didn't want a child who reminded her that there had been another lady in her place before, that the hurried nature of their union had caused a minor scandal. She treated me like an afterthought and my father, sadly, followed suit. I was very lonely until Alice was born. And then I fell in love with her."

He smiled. "A living doll."

"At first, yes," she said. "I even dressed her in my dolly clothes until she got too big. But eventually it became clear Prudence wasn't all that interested in being a mother. She had no warmth when it came to Alice any more than she did with me and left her to the care of servants. Not all that uncommon, I suppose, of women of her station, but I could see Alice wanted more affection. So I gave it. Alice used to playfully call me Little Mama. Until Prudence found out." Her voice got far away like she was reliving that moment. "She was *so* angry."

He shook his head, anger on her behalf rising sharp and strong in his chest. "I'm so sorry, Lily. For both of you. But why does she continue to harangue you now?"

"Oh, Lockhart, this isn't your trouble, is it? You have enough on your mind and—"

"You know it's my trouble," he interrupted, and his heart throbbed when she met his gaze. When she licked her lips and her hands fisted at her sides with the fight they were both waging. "You can pretend that it's for the sake of my future wife if it helps."

She looked up toward the house again and her breath was shaky before she continued, "Prudence tells me I'm making everyone look at me. That I'm trying to be the center of attention like a selfish wretch."

His jaw set. "She called you that? When she has no idea what you are trying to do, trying to create for your sister?"

She shrugged. "She isn't so far off the mark, though, is she? If she knew what happened between you and I...she might kill me."

He wasn't certain if she was being genuine in that statement or not, but his stomach turned at the idea. "You could *never* be selfish, Lily. And if everyone looks at you it's because you are so...so very bright. Like sunshine that parts the clouds and suddenly the world is warm and dazzling and perfect."

Her lips parted and her gaze lifted to his. She was so entirely beautiful that all he wanted to do was touch her. Cup her cheek, tilt her face even further toward his own, kiss her and forget that anything else in the world existed.

He might have at that. Whatever grip he had on control seemed to waver when he came within ten feet of her. But she was stronger. She stepped back and turned away slightly. "When you look at me that way it makes this impossible, George."

She used his given name and he'd never loved it more. Or hated it more because it wouldn't last.

"I know. I'm sorry." He stepped back and smoothed his hands over his jacket. "Would you like me to intervene on your behalf with Lady Westinghouse?"

She shook her head. "That would certainly make it worse, though I appreciate your thought to play knight in shining armor. No, it's best for me just to get through this. Once you and Alice..." She trailed off and drew a trembling breath. "Once you and Alice are married, then I'll be free of her mother. I can visit my sister when Prudence isn't around and our relationship will no longer be dictated by her whims and cruelties."

"That I promise you," he said softly, and hated it was all he could give her.

She didn't look at him. "You should go back inside. You'll be missed."

"Yes." He smoothed his clothing again like he could wipe the effect of her away even though that was impossible. She lingered like a perfume on his skin. He started away from her with great difficulty, but then turned back. "I do understand what it's like to try to live up to impossible standards. For what it's worth, I see you, Lily."

Her breath hitched. "To be seen? That's worth a great deal. Thank you."

He didn't respond, but left her. Went back into the house. Tried to forget the encounter, tried to forget the increased intimacy her soft confessions had created.

And knew he couldn't. Just as he couldn't forget anything else between them.

CHAPTER 13

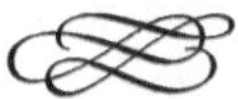

The days that passed after the ball should have been called successful by Lily. After all, having the others in the house had filled the rooms not just with laughter and warmth, but it had allowed her to avoid moments alone with Lockhart. Esme intervened from time to time, drawing Lily away when she couldn't stop watching him. Changing the subject subtly when the topic of the wedding caused Lily's stomach to churn.

And Lockhart was doing his part, as well. She watched as he tried to connect more with her sister. He seemed to seek her out, spoke to her at further length then before. He even called her Alice now, rather than Miss Westinghouse, when he stood talking to her as he did in that very moment across the parlor from Lily.

It all should have relieved her. It didn't. She still dreamed of the man at night. The passionate dreams she'd come to accept, but it was the ones where he was just there with her that hurt more now. Dreams where he put an arm around her as they walked through the garden or pushed a lock of hair away from her face before he leaned in. She woke just as he would kiss her and it broke her heart every time.

Tears stung her eyes and she drew a harsh breath before she blinked them away.

"They look well together, don't they?"

She realized that Lady Pembrooke had approached and now stood with her, watching the couple.

Clearing her throat so her voice wouldn't sound strangled, Lily said, "Yes. They do make a beautiful pair."

It was true. Alice's fairness made a lovely contrast to Lockhart's dark features. They were both beautiful and when they were married and entered a room, she had no doubt people would stare at them. Comment on the viscount and how he had caught himself a stunning bride.

"Better than how pretty she is, your sister is lovely on the inside," Lady Pembrooke said, facing Lily slightly.

That compliment *did* erase Lily's more painful feelings and her chest swelled with pride at the statement. "Thank you, my lady. She truly is. Alice is kind and bright. She's shy, but that will likely improve with age and as she gains further experience in the world."

"Yes. I think I have also come to understand that your sister's graces are perhaps more to do with *your* influence than anything else." Lady Pembrooke glanced at Prudence. Lily's stepmother was with Marianne near the fireplace, and she was talking incessantly. Marianne nodded, but it was clear she wasn't getting a word in edgewise, but was too kind to orchestrate an escape.

Lily caught her breath. She'd explained her history with Prudence to Lockhart just a few days before and now Lady Pembrooke referenced it. She feared that wasn't a coincidence. "Did…did Lockhart tell you that?"

Lady Pembrooke's eyebrows lifted at the question and she looked again toward her son and then back at Lily. "No," she said slowly. "I simply see it. And the way Alice speaks about you implies it, as well."

"Oh." She feared she'd revealed too much of herself to this woman and so she remained quiet as they returned to watching the couple. At last Alice turned away from him, her mouth curving down the moment she didn't believe he could see. Lockhart let out a small sigh before he stepped away to join some of the others.

Her heart both soared and sank. Sank because their lack of connection could only bring heartbreak to them both. Soared because…well, because she was selfish, wasn't she? No matter what George said to the contrary, what she was feeling was grasping for what wasn't hers just because she'd held it for one perfect night.

"I don't know if I did the right thing," Lady Pembrooke breathed.

Lily wrinkled her brow as she looked at Lady Pembrooke's troubled expression. "How so?"

Instead of answering, the countess's face went pale and she swayed a fraction. Lily caught her arm, shoring her up. "Oh my lady, gracious, are you well? Here, let me take you to the settee."

"Thank you," Lady Pembrooke said, her voice suddenly very small.

"Oh, Aunt Louisa," Clarissa gasped, breaking away from her husband to move across the room toward them. Lord Pembrooke had been standing with the other earls and he also began across the room, his expression concerned.

But it was Lockhart whose reaction was most powerful. He'd been at the sideboard refreshing his drink, but he pivoted when Clarissa called out and there was such an expression on his face as Lily helped his mother to a seat. Something ragged and raw, horror and terror, but all of it laced with a pain that she recognized and felt too keenly.

Heartbreak. Loss.

As he rushed across the room toward them, practically bowling over his father as he did so, Lily looked at Lady Pembrooke. It wasn't the first time she'd noticed the countess seemed…off, somehow. Now she wondered what was wrong with her. And why only Lockhart seemed to be so truly terrified of it.

He took a place next to his mother, catching her hand in both of his. "Mama, are you well?"

She nodded, though the color hadn't returned to her cheeks. "Oh, yes. Just a little dizzy. It's all the excitement, I suppose."

Lockhart glanced up at Lily, his eyes still wild. In that moment she desperately wanted to put her hand on his shoulder. To give him support. She had to clench a fist at her side to keep from doing just that and showing the entire room emotions that were just as deep and dangerous as his fear.

Lily stepped away as Lord Pembrooke sat down on his wife's other side. His face was lined with worry and confusion at this unexpected moment. "Why don't I escort you upstairs, Louisa? I'll have food brought up and you can rest a bit, I'm sure the crowd will understand."

There were affirmative murmurs all around from the others. Lady Pembrooke rose with the help of her husband, only releasing her son's hand when she was on her feet. Lord Pembrooke put an arm around her and as she insisted on saying her apologies, he guided her from the room.

The moment they were gone, Lockhart shook his head and strode from the room behind them, though he turned the opposite way from his parents. Lily's lips parted at his sudden departure. He hadn't even said a word to the others, despite all of them being family and dear friends. More than ever, she knew something very deep and dark was wrong here, and she felt more powerfully than before that she wanted to comfort him. She *needed* to do so.

"What was *that* about?" Esme said, breaking the spell.

Clarissa was staring at the door where her aunt and uncle had gone and shook her head. "I'm not certain. Aunt Louisa is right, there is a great deal of excitement. Perhaps that's all it is."

Lily let out a shaky breath. "I-I have noticed her wobble a few times since my arrival."

Clarissa's lips parted with surprise. "Oh."

"Lockhart looked sick with worry," Lord Kirkwood said as he stepped up to Clarissa to take her hand briefly.

"Yes, he did," Lily answered, even though the statement hadn't been made toward her.

"Perhaps I should go after him," Kirkwood said, and exchanged a meaningful look with his wife. "Try to get to the bottom of it."

She nodded. "Would you? I think he needs a friend more than his cousin at present."

"I'd say you are his friend, as well, love, but I'll go. I'll drag these two along with me." He motioned to Ramsbury and Delacourt.

"With pleasure," Ramsbury said. "I wonder if he went for a ride."

"Or perhaps down to the lake?" Delacourt suggested as the three of them started from the parlor together.

As Clarissa, Marianne and Esme continued to talk together, Lily realized that Prudence and Alice weren't in their group. She hadn't expected her stepmother to join. She was at the sideboard pouring whisky in her tea and looked annoyed that the gathering had been interrupted. Of course she would. She had no ability to have compassion for others.

But Alice surprised Lily more, for she had a deep well of kindness under normal circumstances. But *she* was standing at the window, looking out with a pensive expression. Lily made her way to her sister.

"Do you think Lady Pembrooke is well?" Alice asked.

Lily pursed her lips and thought again of the terror in Lockhart's expression. "I-I don't know."

"I hope so. She's very kind." There was a pause. "But...but if she's not, perhaps we should postpone the wedding."

There was almost...*hope* in her sister's tone at that idea and Lily stiffened at it. Every time she saw evidence of Alice's lack of interest in the marriage, she felt such a shot of yearning laced with horror at the consequences.

"I don't know that we're at that stage yet," she said gently. "Do you think perhaps you should go speak to Lockhart?"

Alice jolted and glanced up at her. "Oh. I suppose he did seem upset, didn't he? But is that really my place?"

Lily blinked at that question. Could her sister truly be so innocent? "He'll be your husband in a very short time, Alice. To support him is *exactly* your place. That connection, that encouragement between partners is at the core of the best marriages. You must see that when you look at all our friends."

If she hoped Alice would take that advice in, she was disappointed. Rather than that, her sister looked shocked. A little like a fox cornered by hounds. Her expression twisted and her hands shook before she shoved them behind her back.

"Oh, Lily," Alice said softly. "Please…I don't know. I can't, please don't ask me…"

The tears that filled her sister's eyes made Lily's heart drop further. Even this reasonable suggestion created too much of a bond to the man for Alice. And here was Lily, longing to find him, to uncover his pain, to wrap her love around it so that it stung less.

For the first time in her life, Lily resented Alice for not embracing what Lily wanted so much. How could her sister not love this man? How could she not connect with him at all when he was everything a person could ever want?

"Well, if you don't think you can, it's fine," she lied. "I'm sure you'll learn as you come to know him better over the years."

Alice nodded. Lily stepped back from her and smoothed her hands over her skirt, the need to find Lockhart filling every part of her being. The men were going to look for him and she should have let that be.

But she feared the places they sought him wouldn't be the places he'd be found. She knew where he would go in this moment of pain and worry. And then she was moving, almost against her own will, slipping from the room as the others continued to talk quietly.

She left the room and the house and made her way to him, knowing it was a mistake and not giving a damn.

~

George stood in the darkness of the tower, his hands pressed to the cold stone of the interior walls and he couldn't breathe. The reality of everything happening in his life was hitting him and it felt like shotgun blasts that knocked him back over and over again.

His mother had looked so small as she sat on the settee, pale and trembling. She'd always been such a big presence in his life, such a warm light, and now he felt her dimming. Fading.

And in her place would be Alice. Alice, who would hardly look at him. Alice, who clearly had no interest in him. His marriage would be empty, cold, and all he would have were memories of Lily to keep him warm.

Worse, Lily would come to his home. She would spend time with her sister. They would look at each other over tables and all he would feel was this pulse of desire and longing for her that he was beginning to realize would never fade away.

He looked into that future and it all seemed so hopeless and empty. And unavoidable.

"Lockhart?" He heard the sound in the distance and squeezed his eyes shut. He was either hearing Lily's voice now in his distress or he had actually conjured her to him in this moment of pain. He remained quiet, hoping she wouldn't appear.

Praying she would.

"Lockhart?" Her voice came again and then after a pause, "George?"

He let out a shaky breath and stepped from the tower into the brilliant sunshine of the afternoon. "Lily?"

She jolted as she saw him and rushed toward him, hands clenched at her sides. She lifted them toward him and then hesitated. A caress not given and yet he still felt it like she'd moved those same hands over his skin. It was torture.

"I was worried about you," she said.

He stared at her, this woman who had come to rescue him from a tower. This woman whose gentle kindnesses and heated passions seemed to intertwine with his with ease, as if they were meant to do so. He stared at her and all he wanted to do was take her back into the cool building behind them, lock them both in, and pretend the rest of the world no longer existed.

"I'm well," he croaked out instead. "I needed air."

She held his gaze, searching there. Seeing, he feared. Of course she would see, she held the keys to everything didn't she? And he was too weak to resist her, especially now.

"George," she said, her voice shaking. "Why did you decide to marry my sister?"

That should have felt like a change of subject, but they both knew it wasn't. He had the explanations to why, but he had no idea how she'd guessed. How she'd probed into the heart of him and plucked out a bitter truth with such little effort.

He turned his head so she'd no longer be able to delve so deeply into his soul. He needed the lie now, at least to attempt it. "It was time and—"

She moved closer. "No. You didn't choose her. It's clear you didn't."

He sucked in a few heavy breaths. "I implore you, Lily, don't ask these questions. I cannot do this."

There was a brief knife's edge of time when he didn't know if she would retreat or advance. When he hoped and wasn't certain what outcome he hoped for. Then she moved forward once more and took his hand and he knew.

He wanted to tell her.

Her fingers were warm on his, gentle as she lifted his hand and kissed his knuckles. "Why, George? Why do this? And why so rushed when there seems to be no pleasure to be found for either party?"

His stomach turned and the only thing keeping him grounded was her touch. He gripped her hand tighter and met her eyes, knowing his looked as wild as he felt inside as the truth threatened to hatch like some hideous beast from an egg. If he let it loose it would rampage.

And yet he could no longer hold it in.

"Because...because my mother...my mother is sick," he whispered, and the tears began to sting his eyes. "Because she's dying, Lily. And all she wants is to see me settled before that day comes."

CHAPTER 14

It was odd how saying those words out loud created two instant reaction reactions in George. The first was horror. He had set the truth free, put it on the wind and made it real in a way he'd been trying to suppress.

But there was also relief. Since his mother had told him of her illness months ago, since she'd pleaded with him to marry so that she would know he was settled, he had carried that secret. It was theirs, his and his mother's, and yet it was his weight, pressing down on his shoulders.

"Oh, Lockhart, I'm so sorry." Lily cupped both of his cheeks gently, bringing him back to this moment, this reality. She wiped one of his tears away with her thumb as she gazed up into him and somehow made it all...better, for the first time in months. He wanted more of that, foolish and selfish as that desire was.

"She told me right around the time Clarissa and Kirkwood wed," he continued, his voice rough in the quiet. "The doctor told her there was nothing to do, that there was no guessing how much time she has left, but it cannot be long."

Because she had already told him she'd lost her mother, he saw the understanding her gaze. "But your cousin and your father don't seem to know about this?" she said softly.

"She didn't want to mar Clarissa's happiness after so many years of struggle. And as for my father…" He shook his head. "I think she fears it being proven that he doesn't care."

"Because of their past. Because of his infidelities."

He nodded. "Even though it's been years."

"*Do* you think he cares?" she asked.

He hesitated. "I do. In so much as he can."

"I know their relationship has been fraught, though he seems attentive to her now."

He pressed his lips together. "Yes," he admitted slowly. "I see that too. A few years ago they seemed to come to an accord of sorts. It's…hard for me to accept it after everything else. It must be for her, too."

She nodded slowly. "I can understand that fear on her part."

He knew she did. God, she understood all of this and it suddenly felt like he had an ally to roll this terrible weight up the hill.

"When she told me, I was shocked. Heartbroken." His voice broke and he swallowed. "I asked her what I could do, how I could ease her pain. She said that she wished to see me wed. Settled like my friends all were."

"But why not court your own lady?" Lily asked. "Find someone you had a connection to."

"I was so rocked by her news, I couldn't picture pursuing someone like that. She suggested that she might find me an arrangement. She had a list of potentials, just three names. Two I knew and had no interest in, and that left Alice. Who is kind and lovely and everything I *should* want."

"But you don't," she said softly. "Even before me."

He nodded. "I *have* tried, but these last few weeks have proven at last that it's hopeless. And yet what can I do? There is hardly any time before the wedding and my mother is still ill, perhaps more gravely than I believed given today's collapse. To end the engagement would cause ruination and scandal to both our names. And harm my mother and all her hopes."

He paced away from her and the touch that soothed and yet still burned. "I am trapped. I have walked into that trap willingly to soothe a much beloved mother and what will happen at the end of this road? She'll be lost regardless—"

He broke off as the wave of pain washed over him, more powerfully than he had ever allowed it before. He staggered to his knees in the broken remnants of the castle halls and howled the pain into the air where it floated away.

Lily was there then, down on her knees beside him, her arms coming around him, bringing his head to her shoulder as he wept with an intensity he hadn't experienced since he was a very young child. She whispered gentle, meaningless words of comfort and protection, her hands smoothing along his back as she held him.

At last the cloud passed, the pain receded a fraction, the weight returned to his shoulders, though with less pressure than it had been before. He lifted his head and they sat in the grass, looking at each other.

"I'm sorry," he said.

She smoothed a lock of hair away from his forehead. "You shouldn't be. This is such a hurt, George. How could you carry it alone?"

"But I shouldn't give it to you, Lily." He took her hand and lifted it to his lips just as she had done with his. "Not *you*. It's wretchedly unfair of me. Entirely selfish."

"But I *do* understand it," she said. "And I am glad to know the whole story. To realize at last why all this happened in such a rush."

The rush. God, that was the rub, wasn't it? If he and his mother hadn't rushed all this for the sake of fulfilling her last wish, he wouldn't have been in quite so deep with Alice when he met Lily at the masquerade. He would have had the opportunity to find her in his own way, to get to know her...to have the future that was now snatched from him.

Everything would have been different.

Now he was left with the reality that the only person in the world he wanted to tell his secrets, the painful or the joyful, was the woman sitting on the grass beside him. He wanted to be able to ask her to bear his pain and know it wasn't unfair, because he would do the same for her with pride. Because he loved her. He *loved* Lily and it wasn't even a surprise to him to recognize it.

He touched her cheek gently, memorizing all the gorgeous lines of her, all the warm emotions in her eyes, all the edges and curves of her. She truly was a goddess, just as she had been in those first moments he'd met her. But he didn't want to be a god of war who lost her. He wanted to be her acolyte. To follow behind her, worshipping at her feet for the rest of his days.

She made a soft sound as his fingers dragged along her skin and he found himself leaning into her. The rest of the world fell away as she turned her face upward and their lips drew closer. Close enough that he could feel her breath.

With a gasp, she turned away and he was dragged back to reality. To all the reasons why a kiss between them now would be world breaking. He rested his forehead against her shoulder a moment, both of them breathing raggedly in the quiet.

At last, she got up and dusted off her gown. He watched her from his place on the ground a moment before he joined her on his feet.

"I am...I'm truly sorry, my lord," she said softly, not meeting his eyes once more.

He nodded. "Thank you."

"I won't—I won't say anything to anyone about what you told me," she promised, and then she did lift her gaze to him. "But may I suggest that it might help if you weren't the one carrying all this burden? There are so many up at that house who...who *love* you, Lockhart. Their concern when you left them was so clear, as clear as their worry for your mother. I think all of them would be glad share in some of this burden."

"You mean, I suppose, that the secret can burn as much as the injury," he said.

She looked at him and for a moment there was only silence between them before she nodded. "Yes. I'll leave you to the tower, my lord. Good day."

"Good day," he said, and watched her walk away, her steps as unsteady as his aching heart.

~

If Lockhart and his mother had told any of the other family about her illness, Lily couldn't see evidence of it in the days that followed his confession at the tower. Everyone continued to behave normally, including Lady Pembrooke, who returned to the gathering by the next day as if nothing had happened.

Certainly, Lily didn't think he had confided in Alice, either. Her sister would have told her if he had, for Alice hadn't ever been very good at keeping secrets. Her open face revealed too much.

So it was, it seemed, still something he'd shared with her alone. Another private bond that only added to the weight of regrets on her shoulders. A reminder of what could never be.

As was her sister. Alice stood on the dais before a full-length mirror with her seamstress darting around her, adding the final tucks and pins for her wedding gown. Lily pushed her other thoughts away and focused instead on how beautiful her sister was. The gown was the finest silk and lace, with just hints of pink along the bodice that would have made the color in Alice's cheeks pop if her sister *had* any color in those cheeks. At present, she didn't. She just stared at herself in the mirror, her face drawn down in a deep frown.

Lily stepped toward her. "You do look beautiful, my love."

That seemed to shake Alice whatever thoughts troubled her and she glanced over her shoulder at Lily with a smile. "Thank you. Did you…did you say that you brought in your gowns to have me look at?"

Lily hesitated at her sister's question. Alice was definitely troubled if she wasn't clear about a conversation they'd had less than a quarter hour before when Lily had first arrived in the room, dresses draped over her arm.

"I did," she said gently. "I brought two with a thought to wear one of them on your wedding day. One has a very similar pink to the highlights of your gown."

"How did you know there was pink in it?" Alice asked, lifting her arm so the seamstress could mark something along her side.

"Mary told Susan," Lily explained.

"Mary did?" There was something a little wistful to her sister's tone, but when she continued speaking it was gone. "I suppose she would, as they are cousins."

"I wasn't certain you wished to have me match you, though. It might take away from you, or at least that's what your mother might say."

"Mother can keep her opinions to herself," Alice said with uncharacteristic heat. "I love the idea of you having that little connection to me. It will make me less nervous. Will you put it on so we can stand next to each other in the mirror and see if we like the effect?"

"Certainly," Lily said and gathered up the dress. "May I borrow Mary so I don't have to ring for Susan?"

"Yes. She should be in the dressing room through there," Alice said, motioning across the room. "I think she was putting some things away from the laundering this morning."

"I'm surprised she could keep herself from observing the fitting. You two are so close."

Her sister didn't answer but went back to staring into the mirror and so Lily went into the dressing room. She found Mary sitting on a chair within, matching stockings. When she lifted her gaze, her eyes were a little puffy, as if she'd been crying.

"Oh, Mary, I didn't mean to interrupt," Lily said.

The young woman got up immediately and set the stockings aside. "Of course not, Mrs. Manning. How can I help?"

"Alice wants to see me in this dress alongside her wedding gown. Do you think you could help?"

"Of course."

They were quiet as the maid helped her remove her original gown and put on the pink instead. Mary's fingers faltered a few times, but Lily wasn't certain why. Mary was quite young, of course. Just a year older than her sister, in fact. Perhaps it was just inexperience.

"Are you well, Mary?" Lily asked as the young woman fastened the last few buttons on the dress.

"I…of course, ma'am."

Lily faced her. "You look as though you've been crying. Is there anything I can do to help?"

The young maid dropped her chin and stared at the ground instead of Lily. "Oh, no. You're very kind to offer but there's… there's nothing anyone can do."

"Are you worried about your place after Alice marries?" Lily pressed. There was a long enough hesitation that she realized she had hit upon the truth. She caught Mary's hand gently. "I know you are of great comfort to Alice. She says so often. And Lord Lockhart is very kind. He would never force her to change her servants. I believe with all my heart that your place on staff is safe."

She expected there to be relief on Mary's face at those words, but the trouble remained as the young woman glanced up at her. "Thank you for saying that, ma'am. It's very considerate of you to think of me. Please don't say anything to Alice…to Miss Alice, though. I don't want her to worry about me when she has so many things going on."

Lily smiled at the kindness of that thought. "I won't. Thank you for your help."

Mary went back to her stockings and Lily returned to the main chamber. The seamstress had left the room and Alice remained on the dais, looking in the mirror, her expression blank.

"What do you think?" Lily asked, and Alice jumped before she turned to look at her. Now her face lit up. "Oh my, it almost matches perfectly. Like we were made to stand together."

She motioned Lily to come to her and stepped down from the platform so they could stand at the mirror, arms wrapped around each other. Lily caught her breath. Alice was so much younger than she was, it was sometimes difficult to remember that she was grown except in these moments where she looked so much like a lady.

"Oh, Lily, you are so beautiful," Alice said softly.

Lily ducked her head as tears stung her eyes. "Nothing like you, dearest. You will be so…" She glanced up again, and this time when she looked in the mirror she didn't see her sister but the woman who would marry Lockhart. She pushed her pain and jealousy at that aside. "You will be so perfect on your wedding day."

If she expected Alice to smile or blush, her sister's reaction was shocking. Alice drew in a shaky breath and then, without preamble, began to sob. Great, wracking sobs that shook her shoulders and left tears streaming down her face.

"Oh no," Lily said, putting her arm around her sister more tightly and guiding her to the settee before the fire. They sat together. "What is it, love? What can I do? Are you nervous? Uncertain?"

Alice lifted her head and the tears continued to flow, even as she choked out, "Uncertain? Oh no, I'm perfectly certain. Lily, I don't want to marry him."

And there it was, the words Lily had known in her heart that Alice felt, finally spoken aloud. But knowing they had been there, waiting to be spilled, wasn't the same was hearing them. As having them hit her in the chest like a punch.

She took Alice's hands in hers. It was so unfair that it had to be Lily who be the one to do this. To convince her sister to carry on with something that would ultimately cause her own heartbreak.

"This is an arrangement and of course that can be frightening," she said softly. "But George—Lockhart, he is a *good* man. He wouldn't ever hurt you and he'll look after you in the ways a husband should. If you open your heart, you could even come to… come to love him."

Her sister's face twisted in what appeared to be horror and she snatched her hands away. "Love him?" she repeated. "You say that because you were so happy, but that won't be me, Lily. I do not love Lockhart and I shall *never* love him. Not like I love—"

She broke off and got to her feet, pacing away to the window. But Lily had heard and understood perfectly the truncated sentence that now hung in the air between them.

She got up slowly. "Alice, are you in love with another man?"

Her sister stood still at the window a moment, but then she turned back. "No."

That didn't appear to be a lie. Alice was calm and quiet now, the upset that had torn at her pushed back down, along with whatever secret she had been about to tell.

Alice drew in a few shaky breaths. "I-I'm sorry. I shouldn't have allowed that outburst. You are right that I'm simply nervous and behaving irrationally."

"I don't think I ever said-"

"Why don't you let me change and have a moment to regather myself?"

Lily opened and shut her mouth, uncertain what to say or do now. How to help her sister when the wheels of this were in motion, almost out of control. It was too late to turn them back…wasn't it?

"Of course, I'll let you have a moment. On my way out, I'll fetch Mary to help you."

Alice ducked her head again. "Thank you."

Lily went to the dressing room and opened the door once more. "Mary, Alice will need help changing."

If Mary had looked upset before, now she had pushed those emotions away. She looked past Lily, almost as if she could see Alice. "Of course," she said, and got up to do her duty.

Lily left the chamber and shut the door. As she walked down the long hallway back toward her own chamber, she was flooded with all the awful feelings of this situation. Both her sister and George had confessed to being trapped into this marriage. Both would suffer if he happened.

And yet was she the one who should make that point? Because she was not a disinterested party. There were entirely selfish reasons for her to wish the engagement ended. Were her own needs enough reason to call for a scandal that would harm everyone involved? Was there no way the two of them could find some happiness?

She was about to enter her chamber to ponder that further, but when she looked down to grasp the door handle, she realized she was still wearing the pink gown. She'd left not only her second option, but her original dress back in her sister's room.

She rolled her eyes at the distraction that had been caused by all the high emotions and headed back to Alice's chamber. She gave a light knock before she opened the door.

She expected to see Mary helping Alice dress, but what she saw inside instead brought her up short.

Alice was still on the settee in her wedding dress and Mary sat with her, arms around her. Mary was stroking her hair gently as Alice buried her head in her maid's shoulder. Neither noticed Lily there, they were so wrapped up in whatever was between them.

Lily had an odd feeling in her stomach, even though it seemed this was just a friend comforting a friend. They were of an age and had grown up around each other, Alice hadn't learned yet how to put a little distance between them. She was ready to back away and allow them to have their moment, but then Alice turned her face toward Mary and whispered, "I hate this. I hate this, my love."

Mary nodded. "I do too, Alice. More than anything."

Then she bent her head and kissed Alice. It was gentle at first, but then Alice made a little sound and lifted into the other woman, her arms coming around her tighter.

Lily covered her mouth before she stepped back and shut the door silently. Her hands shook as she stared in shock at the barrier between herself and whatever was now happening in that room between the two women.

Passion. *Love.* That was what it was. She recognized it because she had felt both of those things herself. Along with the same desperation that had lingered between the two women when they touched. She realized that when Alice had cut herself off when she said she loved another, it hadn't been another man. It had been *Mary.* That one piece of information locked into place and made the picture entirely clear. It also made one other fact just as evident: to go forward with this marriage would be far more devastating than to end it, for all parties.

"I cannot let her do this," Lily said to herself, and it only made her even more certain of that truth.

She pivoted and walked down the hallway toward Prudence's chamber. She needed to stop this, for all their sakes. She only hoped there was a way to do so before all involved were broken beyond repair.

CHAPTER 15

When Prudence answered Lily's desperate knock at her chamber door, it was with annoyance.

"You needn't bang the door down," she snapped as she stepped back to allow Lily into the antechamber. "What do you want? I'm having tea. By myself, I add, since there apparently isn't a gathering this afternoon. Rather cheap of the family, I think."

Lily ignored the scree of nasty comments as she shut the door behind her. "Prudence, I need to speak to you about Alice."

Her stepmother didn't offer her tea, but folded her arms in further displeasure. "I'm sure you have nothing to say. *I* am her mother, not you, no matter what you think."

Lily drew a shaky breath and tried to maintain her calm. As much as Prudence's cruelty shook her, she hadn't seen it often pointed at Alice. No, Prudence mostly ignored her daughter, but when she did pay attention, it was to push her to the forefront. To try to obtain the best through her. But perhaps she truly did care for her at that.

Lily clung to that idea, even if she deeply doubted its veracity. "I- I was just with Alice for her final fitting of her wedding gown."

"Lovely, isn't it?" Prudence said with a thin, cruel smile. "I spared *no* expense. Were you jealous it was far finer than your own to Manning? Honestly, your sister is marrying a viscount and will one day be countess. Why *shouldn't* I spend more on her?"

"You must know I care nothing for that," Lily said. "Alice deserves lovely things and she looks beautiful. But you cannot be unaware of how unhappy she is with this match, Prudence."

Her stepmother's lips tightened. "What do you mean?"

"You watch her as I do, don't you? You see how she has no connection to Lockhart. You see how she is always on the edge of collapse. You *must* see it. She's never been very good about keeping the truth from her expression."

Though now Lily doubted that statement. Certainly Alice had done a fine job of hiding her true feelings for Mary.

"She will be happy enough when she has a fortune to spend and an estate to enjoy," Prudence said. "We *all* make sacrifices for our futures. Do you think I loved your father?"

Lily flinched, for if Prudence hadn't loved him, he had certainly loved her. He'd sacrificed his oldest daughter to make her happy. Chosen her over Lily every time he was offered the opportunity until the day he died.

"If you didn't, then you must know, as I do, how empty that sort of union can be. You cannot want that for her, not with her romantic, sweet disposition. The wedding is still weeks away—could we not at least hold it to allow further discussion on this matter? Please, think of Alice's happiness and well-being."

Her stepmother's nostrils flared and without warning her hand shot out. She slapped Lily so hard that her head turned and her cheek immediately stung so much that tears came to her eyes. She covered the heat of it with her palm and stared in shock at Prudence.

It wasn't that it was the first time it had happened. But Prudence hadn't struck her since she was a child.

"Don't pretend you care about her happiness," Prudence hissed. "You care about yourself. About having *him* for yourself."

Lily staggered back, hand still pressed against her cheek. She must have heard that wrong. Misunderstood. But how could she misunderstand? Prudence was perfectly clear.

"I-I don't know what you're talking about," she said.

Prudence stepped forward and it took every ounce of strength in Lily to maintain her position as her stepmother pressed closer, her eyes lit with rage and her hands trembling. "I *saw* you two at that rundown tower."

It felt like Lily's heart stopped beating, her blood stopped moving, the world stopped turning as she stared at Prudence. There was no doubt Prudence was referring to her and Lockhart. There had been two times she'd been at the tower with him. The first was when they'd toured it originally after he discovered who she was. The second when he'd broken down about his mother and they'd nearly kissed.

Both had been moments of high emotion and intimacy, even if they hadn't given in to the feelings between them. Neither was a scenario where she would have wanted to be seen by anyone, but most especially this woman.

"When?" she whispered.

Prudence's eyes widened. "Oh, were there more assignations than when he took you on your little tour? Did you spread your legs for him in the dirt there while your sister slept in her bed not a quarter mile up the lane?"

"No!" Lily gasped out. "I would *never* do that to her."

"Why not? You certainly must want to marry a man of such title and fortune."

Lily gripped her hands at her sides. Her stepmother was so entirely blind to reality. She drew a long breath. "Even if that's what you think about me, you must understand that my hesitations aren't about my own desires, Prudence. Please, put your hatred for me aside, put whatever you think of me and how you wish to hurt me aside, and know that I adore Alice. I would *never* interfere for my own sake and I haven't. I only bring this to you because I must believe you love her, too, and want the best for her."

"What do you know about what's best for her?"

"She…she cares for someone else," she said, and nothing further. She wasn't about to say who to Prudence. Her stepmother would be shocked by the truth and it would only make things worse. And it wasn't her secret to reveal. To do so would be just as big a betrayal as her feelings toward Lockhart were.

But Prudence didn't look surprised by the declaration. She tilted her head back and chuckled. "Are you talking about Mary?"

Lily's lips parted in shock. "You…you…"

"Oh, yes, I know all about that. As you said, Alice isn't capable of covering her emotions when they fly to her face. I've known for months. I warned her to put a stop to the wicked affair. I told her what would happen if she didn't do that and then marry this man without argument. Perhaps it's time I fulfill that promise."

"What promise?" Lily whispered, almost fearing the answer because it was clear her stepmother *didn't* care for Alice, after all, or at least not enough to put her first.

"To put Mary out on the street without reference," Prudence said. "And be sure she can do nothing but lie on her back to pay for her bread."

"That…that's blackmail." Lily shook her head. "You—you *black-mailed* Alice with vile threats toward the person she loves?"

"I gave her incentive." Prudence shrugged. "But clearly not enough. So now we will move on to the punitive stage of this agreement."

"No," Lily said, lunging for her arm. "Please, think of what you're doing. What you could cause if you press them. They're desperate already, this could push one or both of them off the edge. You cannot wish to see this end with an avoidable tragedy."

Prudence dug her nails into the hand that held her arm and Lily yelped as the skin tore. When she let go slightly, Prudence shoved her and she tumbled back, crashing partly into the table behind her and falling to the ground. Her cheek slammed against the table edge as she did so and stars lit up before her eyes as pain rocked through her.

"Stay out of it, you little bitch. You've caused more than enough trouble."

Prudence left the room and Lily sat on the floor a moment, trying to regain her faculties. She could taste a tinge of blood in her mouth and her lip and cheek hurt fiercely. But she had to get up. Prudence would harm Alice, perhaps more than she knew, and it was clear now that Lily couldn't stop her alone.

She could think of only one person who could help her now. And he had every reason to make sure this marriage went forward, along with every desire to see it end.

~

Usually George was good at billiards. In fact, he regularly routed Ramsbury, Delacourt and Kirkwood when the men gathered together. But now the group of them stood around his table, laughing and having a drink before they would retire to prepare for supper and he was playing like shite. He felt like it, too.

He snapped the cue against the ball and it went sideways instead of straight, missing all his targets.

He slammed the cue down on the edge of the table. "Bloody fuck."

There was a long silence in the room around him as his friends stopped talking and looked at him. He saw them exchange little glances, little conversations with their eyes. About him. About his bad mood.

About the topic he couldn't broach, not with them, not with anyone, because how could a man explain that he was in love with his intended's sister? That he wanted to be with her every moment of every day, that he could only find her in his dreams and woke yearning all the more? That he was crushed at the idea that they could never be together, but couldn't escape the trap he was now in?

A man couldn't do that and not have everyone he cared for look at him like he was a monster. The entire situation was monstrous, after all.

"Are we ever going to talk about the obvious?" Kirkwood asked softly.

Fuck, here it came. He turned away and took a long swig of his drink. "What? That I'm playing like I learned the game three days ago? I suppose if you'd like to crow, I won't stop you. I've earned the censure."

"That's not it and you know it," Delacourt said, and started around the table toward him.

Before he could reach him, though, and start a conversation that George knew he would lose control of eventually, the door to the billiard room flew open and the object of his adoration and distraction flew inside.

Lily was wearing a beautiful pink gown that reminded him of spring flowers just beginning to bloom. But her face was pale as paper and there was a bruise on her cheek and blood streaked across her lip.

He lunged across the room toward her. "Christ, what happened to you, Lily?"

She was shaking and she caught his forearms with both her hands, staring up into his face with wild eyes. "I need your help. Please, I need your help, Lockhart. Alice…it's Alice…Prudence will destroy her."

The others had moved forward in concern and now they looked at her, looked at him. They didn't have to have the conversation after all. George could see they all knew. Perhaps he'd never been good enough at hiding it from those who knew him well. Those who recognized a man in love because they saw him in the mirror every day.

"Can we assist?" Ramsbury asked gently.

Lily jumped and looked at the three men. She reached up to wipe her lip, but the blood only smeared a little across her pale skin. "No, I'm sorry. I'm so sorry to interrupt."

"Clearly whatever you have to say is important," Delacourt said. "We'll leave you, but if you need help…"

He didn't finish but gave Lockhart a meaningful look before the men left them. Once they were gone, George drew her to the settee.

"No, we can't sit, we need to—"

He pulled a handkerchief from his pocked and dabbed the blood away from her face. She winced slightly but held still as he said, "We *need* to let you calm down a moment, so I can understand what you're talking about." He tried to rein in the rage that bubbled up in his chest as he examined the already blooming bruise on her face. "Who did this to you?"

She dropped her gaze down and her breath was ragged. "I must tell you everything," she said with a shake of her head. "I know I must even if it will cause even more problems. It—it was Prudence."

"Your stepmother did this?" he barked. "I have never liked that woman, but that she would actually harm you—"

"I tried to stop her from going to Alice's chamber. She threw me off of her and I fell," she explained. She touched her own cheek and winced. "Is it very bad?"

"It's already purple," he said. "You won't be able to hide it."

"I don't know that I'll be able to hide anything anymore." She gripped his hand. "Oh God, this will destroy everything, George. I have no idea how to protect you and her at the same time."

"Shhh," he said, hating that she was so upset, that she wasn't making sense when normally she was perfectly clear. "You don't need to worry about protecting me, let me protect you. Tell me why you wanted to stop Prudence from seeing her daughter."

"Alice…Alice is in love with someone else," she whispered.

He drew back in surprise at that statement. Not anger, not jealousy, just surprise. "In love with who?"

"I-I can't tell you," she said. "Please, understand that I trust you, that I know it's unfair to keep you in the dark, but this isn't my secret to tell."

He pondered that moment. For Lily to keep name of his...well, rival was a strong word, wasn't it? He didn't feel any animosity toward this person, no matter who they were. But if she was keeping the truth from him with such anxiety, it likely meant the answer was something she might consider shocking.

"Very well, I respect that," he said softly.

"You—you do?" she asked. "You wouldn't push for the truth?"

He shrugged. "If it mattered to me, I suppose I might. Though it would be more fair to go directly to Alice about it. But we both know it doesn't. We both know why."

She lifted those beautiful eyes to his. "So you wouldn't hate her for this."

"That would be more than a bit hypocritical of me, wouldn't it? Considering my own...*our* own...situation."

He realized he'd just alluded to the fact that he was in love with her. Her breath hitched and she ducked her gaze away. He refocused on the very serious situation at hand.

"I assume you just realized this fact. That she has another love?"

She nodded. "I-I saw something that proved it."

He blinked. *Saw* something? As far as he knew, Lily's afternoon had been spent with her sister, having the final fittings done for Alice's wedding gown. How she would see something that would reveal Alice's true love was fascinating. Perhaps a letter from the other suitor? Or the suitor himself had made some kind of surprise appearance like Romeo beneath a window?

He cleared his throat. "And after you saw it, did you reveal the truth to your stepmother?"

"Yes, but not the details of who. It turned out she already knew. She used that knowledge to blackmail Alice into marrying you, to keep her...to keep the person my sister was in love with from being harmed."

George recoiled at the idea of such cruelty and manipulation. It explained so much. Alice had always tried, it was clear she did, but he caught her forlorn looks. Her strain. He'd been so caught up in his own dramas that he hadn't thought to explore hers.

Likely because he didn't love her any more than she did him. They were both in love with someone they felt they couldn't have. And that truth suddenly offered a lifeline.

"Seeing my sister so devastated, I thought to press my step-mother to hold off the wedding," Lily continued, her voice a little calmer now. "At least give us all time to work this situation out. But Prudence lashed out and went off to punish them both."

"Bollocks," he said, and got up.

She followed. "I know you feel you must marry Alice because of your mother's illness. And I've supported that despite my own feelings."

He looked at her when she said *feelings*, dancing around the edge of what he already knew when he looked into her eyes. But she kept going. "But while I would not harm her by taking her future, nor would I harm her by allowing someone else to do the same. You must see that this cannot happen now."

He let out a shaky breath. "It would be one thing to marry by arrangement, but marrying by blackmail is unconscionable. At the very least, we must bring all this into the light. Perhaps not who your sister loves, I would not force her to reveal that secret if she didn't wish it, but to have an honest discussion at last and determine what is best for everyone. Even if it means scandal or a broken contract."

Lily sagged a little, relief plain on her beautiful face. "Then we must go up and stop Prudence."

"You'll stay here. I won't have you put into a situation where she might attack you again," he said.

She shook her head. "No. I'll come with you."

He wanted to argue, but he could see there was no time. His Lily was a stubborn one. So he took her hand instead and they fled the room together, up the stairs. He could hear faint sounds of voices from above, which meant they were likely raised. Lily's hand tightened in his at the sound.

"No," she murmured.

"We'll make it right," he promised as they finished climbing the stairs and turned toward Alice's door. Lady Westinghouse was already exiting and her expression was smug. In that moment, George hated this woman. Hated her for forcing her daughter into a life she didn't want, hated her for harming Lily as a child, hated her for hurting her today, both emotionally and physically.

He pushed that hate down and released Lily's hand as he stepped up to her. "Lady Westinghouse," he began.

She looked at him and then past him to Lily. Her eyes narrowed and he found himself shifting to put his body in front of hers as protection. "If you are aware of any problem, my lord, because of interfering family members, I can assure you that it is taken care of. You needn't trouble yourself."

He stepped forward but she widened her stance and blocked the door. "Lady Westinghouse, what have you done?" he asked.

She thrust her shoulders back and lifted her chin haughtily. "*I* have ensured you a fine wife with a good pedigree, my lord. And I have kept both our families from scandal. You ought to thank me, rather than listen to my whore of a stepdaughter who is only trying to turn you with her charms all while she claims to love her sister."

He stepped closer again. "Have a care, my lady," he said softly. "You have no idea of what you speak and I won't have you disparage Mrs. Manning that way."

Her eyes snapped with anger. "You do not want her disparaged even while it seems you have defiled her and the honor of my daughter? Do you not think that could come out if you choose to pursue a path that violates our marriage agreement?"

"Prudence!" Lily gasped behind him.

He ignored her and leaned even closer. He was more than a head taller than Lady Westinghouse and he loomed above her. "Do you want to tangle with me, my lady. Truly? You will find I'm much harder to blackmail than an eighteen-year-old child who wants desperately to please you and save her love."

"So you know of her love. How she has these filthy feelings for another woman. And worse yet her own maid!"

George glanced at Lily and found she had covered her cheeks with her hands. She was trembling at the cruel revelation of her sister's most private secret. He could understand why, for Society hadn't very liberal views on such things. He, on the other hand, was a rake. He had seen a great many ways that love, both physical and emotional, was made. It wasn't a surprise to him. He certainly didn't judge Alice for it. He actually wanted to protect her even further, not just for Lily's sake but for her own.

"Neither Alice nor I have anything to be sorry for, my lady. We have done no harm to anyone."

Lady Westinghouse's eyes narrowed, but he saw the flicker of her fear. "Would your parents say the same, my lord? Would they not be humiliated at your actions if they were to come out."

"I once paraded drunk and naked through Hyde Park on a day of a royal parade," he hissed. "You cannot touch the limits of what and who I am. Now move."

She hesitated, but then stepped aside, folding her arms as he tried the door. It was locked.

"You're being ridiculous," Lady Westinghouse said, smoothing her skirt. "Making something out of nothing."

"Alice," he called out. "Please, it's Lockhart, I would like to talk to you."

Lily stepped up beside him. "You aren't in trouble, dearest, we only want to help. Please unlock the door."

There was no answer.

"She's resting, that's all." Lady Westinghouse shook her head, pretending now that threats and assaults hadn't been of recent memory. "You are both being ridiculous."

"What if she hurt herself?" Lily whispered, and the fear on her face was so plain that it tore at him.

"Alice, please open the door or I shall be forced to break the lock," he called out.

When there was no answer again, he stepped back and then slammed his shoulder into the door near the locking mechanism. It was a thick, finely made thing and he frowned that it hardly gave. He hit it again.

"My lord, you must stop!" Lady Westinghouse cried out. "You are making a scene!"

She wasn't entirely wrong. The sound of him trying to break the door *was* starting to cause commotion in the house. He could hear voices from downstairs, his family and their friends, calling out to find out what was happening. None of it mattered now, not if Lily was right. He could only pray she wasn't.

CHAPTER 16

George's heart pounded in his chest as he stepped back and then rushed to hit the door once again with his shoulder. To his relief, it gave more fully. One more hard hit and it flew open and he staggered partly into the chamber.

Lily rushed past him. "Alice!" she cried out. "Alice!"

But Alice wasn't in the main chamber. Lily looked at the door to the dressing room, which was closed, and her hands shook as she approached it and slowly opened it.

He held his breath, praying that Alice hadn't injured herself out of desperation and heartbreak. But when Lily opened the secondary door, the room was empty.

She trembled with relief, but then faced him. "How could she have gone? We would have seen her."

He motioned to the window. It was wide open and a chair was placed in front of it. They rushed to it together and looked down, but again they weren't met with a broken body and heartache, but only with a little flutter of torn fabric that had caught on a nail as whoever wore it clearly made their way down the tree just outside.

"She's gone?" Lady Westinghouse shrieked.

The others were coming into the room now, his mother and father in the lead. "What's going on? What's happening?"

It was many voices asking the questions, but all George could do was look at Lily. She was staring at the chair where her sister had likely stood to make her escape. He followed her gaze and there was a little scrap of paper with Lily's name on it placed on the seat.

She picked it up and while Lady Westinghouse tried to play off what was happening and the others argued with her behind them, they read it together:

I'm sorry, Lily. Mama says you know about Mary and that you despise me as much as she does for it. I hope that isn't true. Even if it's not, I cannot do this, I cannot lose her. There's no other choice but to run. Alice.

Lily spun on her stepmother and her voice cut through the fray. "You told her that I hated her?"

She lunged and George caught her arms, holding her back against his chest. "No, stop love, stop," he said, close to her ear. "We have to think of Alice now. This woman isn't worth it."

She struggled against him for a moment as Lady Westinghouse cowered like she wasn't the one who had caused Lily's battered face. Finally, George's mother stepped forward.

"What is going on?" she asked, her voice calm against the roar of despair and desperation in the room. That soft, gentle tone seemed to lower the temperature of the room and finally there was quiet so that this situation could be dealt with.

"Thanks to the horrible actions of her wretched mother, Alice has fled," George said through clenched teeth. "Apparently Alice was forced into this marriage. *Blackmailed* into it."

His father gasped and pivoted on Lady Westinghouse with a grimace. "Tell me that isn't true, my lady."

"What is the difference?" Lady Westinghouse said, pushing her shoulders back and giving her head a haughty toss. "An arranged marriage or a forced one. We all want what is best for our houses. I did us all a favor."

Lord Pembrooke's face twisted with further horror at that answer and he turned away from the viscountess in disgust. For all his complicated emotions about his father, George was happy the earl immediately saw the problem in her actions.

"We must find her," Lily said, grasping for his arm. "Please, *please* you must help me."

"We'll *all* help," Esme said. "She couldn't have gone far if this all just happened. Finn, we could take one of the open rigs and search the south fork of the road."

Delacourt looked down at her. "You were uncomfortable in our very fine carriage, Esme. I'm not taking you bouncing along the road in this condition."

"I'll go with Delacourt," Lady Pembrooke said softly and stepped away from her husband and toward the countess. She glanced toward George before he could react. "It is not a question. It's a statement. I will go."

Ramsbury stepped forward. "Marianne and I could take the north."

"If she was on foot, she could go toward the lakes and the tenant fields," Clarissa said. "I know the way very well."

"And you and I will search the wood," George said to Lily. "We'll find her, I swear it."

"Where shall I look?" Lady Westinghouse asked, her voice a little smaller since she realized she was clearly in the role of the villain to the others.

George exchanged a glance with his father and the earl folded his arms. "*You* will stay under the watchful eye of the Countess of Delacourt and I," he said with a little glance at Esme. The young woman looked very up to the task, despite her advancing pregnancy. "So *you* do not cause more pain than you apparently already have."

"Thank you," George said softly as they all made for the hallway. He touched Pembrooke's forearm as they passed by and his father's hand covered his briefly. Delacourt said something to his mother then rushed off to arrange for the rig as the others began to leave the house to do the same, or take their positions in the search.

"I'm so sorry, Lily," Lady Pembrooke said, but she was watching George. "This is clearly a situation that got out of hand. I'll do anything in my power to remedy it once we find Alice."

Lily nodded, even though George could tell she wasn't really seeing his mother. She was too terrified about her sister at present. He leaned in to kiss his mother's cheek and their eyes held for a moment before he put a hand on the small of Lily's back and guided her toward the stairs and hopefully her sister.

Because if they couldn't find Alice, he knew it would shatter the woman he loved and any future that could be had would shatter with her.

~

Lily couldn't breathe as she and George made their way out of the house and down a long and winding path toward the copse of woods in the distance. Her mind raced with every step, her heartbeat pounding in her ears as she pictured her sister's fear that she would lose the person she loved, or cause her harm. Pictured her sister's heartbreak at the idea that Lily could hate her for her heart.

There had been a moment when Lockhart had been trying to break down the door when she had believed her sister might be dead on the floor inside the chamber. Even now she was terrified that the desperation Prudence had created would cause Alice to harm herself before this was all done.

"Lily," George said softly, his hand coming to the small of her back again. His fingers were warm through the silk of her gown and his voice was gentle. "Breathe."

She did as he had instructed, forcing the air in and out of her lungs in a few ragged breaths. That and the warmth of him beside her helped clear her mind and slow the racing of her thoughts and heart. All that had happened became clearer as her emotions calmed.

"You didn't judge her," she whispered.

His brow knitted out of what seemed to be confusion. "For...for what?"

"Loving another woman. For the secret my stepmother was all too happy to reveal."

"Your stepmother is a vicious viper. I judge *her* entirely. But who a person loves? That is their nature. It cannot be changed, even if someone wished to do so, and I don't see anything wrong with it."

She looked at him, her heart swelling even further with this gentle acceptance of Alice. She realized it was a rare thing amongst men of this station. That he would offer it so easily made her adore him even more. "Nor do I. How could I ever? But what is about to happen...what *I* caused...I'm sorry," she managed to choke out as they continued on their way.

He looked down at her from the corner of his eye. "You've nothing to be sorry for. You caused none of this."

She shook her head. "There was more I didn't tell you in my terror about Alice's wellbeing. Prudence...she saw us at the tower. I don't know which time, but neither one is a good time. She thinks I'm trying to break the engagement between you and Alice to steal you."

His nostrils flared ever so slightly and his jaw tightened. "You wouldn't ever harm your sister, even to your own pain. Don't listen to that wretched witch." He was quiet a moment and the fact that he didn't believe that horrible motive of her helped. He swallowed and spoke again at last. "I want to make it clear that I won't force Alice to marry me."

Though Lily was still terrified for her sister, she couldn't pretend that relief didn't rush through her at that sentence, spoken so softly but moving her with such power. She felt all at once like the worst person to have ever existed and like butterfly wings of wild hope now fluttered around her.

She drew a ragged breath. "Prudence may be the wretch you say, but she isn't wrong that to end the engagement will cause a horrible scandal."

He stopped on the path and faced her. "I don't give a damn. I won't hurt Alice by trapping her. She's too precious to you."

She blinked up at him, taking in every line of his face. God, but she did love him. She took his hand as they continued toward the woods. "Did you really get drunk and strip down in the midst of a royal promenade? I heard whispers. That was you?"

"It was," he said. "I did so twelve years ago."

Despite the direness of the situation, she giggled at the idea.

"It wasn't my best hour. Somehow I didn't end up hanged, though, and the gossip rags didn't use my name, even though a large number of people saw it with their own eyes. My survival was my father's doing, I'm sure."

"He loves you," she said softly.

He nodded slowly. "I suppose he does. His immediate disgust at the idea of blackmail being part of the marriage contract, his taking my side no matter what...that is meaningful."

She drew a breath to speak again, but stopped when she saw something with a hint of pink move swiftly at the edge of the wood. She caught his arm with both of hers. "George, I saw something there."

He nodded and then moved forward carefully, hands held up. "Alice if that is you, *please* don't run. We aren't going to do anything to harm you or Mary. Please, trust me."

"Yes, Alice, if you're there, please talk to me," Lily added, hating that her voice cracked with the high emotion. "I would *never* cause you pain on purpose. All I want to do is help you. Keep you and Mary safe."

There was a hesitation and then a rustle in the leaves and

branches. Slowly, Alice and Mary stepped from the cool darkness, their hands intertwined with each other and both their faces pale and drawn.

Lily felt her knees wobble with relief to find her sister unharmed. George caught her elbow and steadied her. Alice stayed at a distance.

"Mama—Mama said you know. That you hate me," she called out and the pain that laced her tone felt so heavy in Lily's chest.

Lily rushed forward a few steps. "Please know I could *never* hate you, but certainly not for who you love!"

At that Alice burst into tears and she released Mary to rush forward into Lily's arms. Lily clung to her as she sagged and wept, smoothing her hair, trying to sooth her fears and hurts just as she had when Alice was little more than a baby.

"Please come back," she said at last.

Alice pulled away at that and took a step back toward Mary. Lily looked at the young woman. The poor girl was shaking like a leaf and kept looking at Lockhart like she thought he would lunge at her at any moment. It was clearly only her deep feelings for Alice kept her from bolting back into the woods. Another point in her favor, that she would be so brave for the woman she loved.

"I can't," Alice said. "Mama sacked Mary and she'll do even worse if we return."

Lockhart shook his head. "I'm sorry that I know your secret, my dear. I'm sorry your mother didn't respect you enough to keep it, to allow you to tell it yourself if you wished to do so." He moved a little closer. "But since I do, I want you both to know that I won't let her do anything to you. And I *won't* separate you two. I promise you that you won't be forced to marry, and Mary will be protected. We'll work this out. But if we don't know where you are, it will be so much harder. On you and on your sister. Please come back to the house."

Now it was Alice and Mary who both wobbled a fraction. Though she glanced at Lily and George, it seemed high emotions overcame secrecy. Mary put her arms around Alice's waist and they clung to each other for a moment before Alice shook her head. "What you must think of me, my lord."

George moved forward, but Lily noted how careful he was, as if he sensed the fear his presence created and didn't want to add to it. "I certainly think nothing less of you in this moment than I did in any other. If anything I think more of you. I also think that all this was rushed forward because of pain. Both yours and mine. But that isn't a reason to marry. I think you're brave to fight for what you want and who you care about."

"But my mother won't let what I want happen," Alice whispered. "Even if you think you can protect me, once the match is broken, she'll have me back under her thumb."

"She won't," George promised. He glanced at Mary again. "Mary, I swear to you that she won't, do you understand?"

Mary finally looked at him and she slowly nodded. "Yes."

"You might not believe me now, but believe your sister, Alice. Believe that we have your best interest and Mary's at heart. And that we won't let anyone harm either of you. But if you run, protecting you will be so much more difficult."

"Please, Alice," Lily said softly. "Please come back and let's work this out together."

Alice looked back at Mary. "What do you want to do?"

Lily smiled a little at that question. Her sister did truly love this woman. Thought of her first. Stared at her with more passion and love and connection than she'd ever shown George, that was certain. That she'd found such a love was truly beautiful. It was everything Lily had hoped for when she dreamed of Alice's future.

"I don't want to ruin your life," Mary whispered, her voice broken.

And now Lily saw the same returned from Mary.

"My life would only be ruined by losing you," Alice said.

Mary sighed. "If you trust him…"

Alice looked at Lily and she nodded, hoping she could turn this tide. At last her sister sighed. "I do."

The words made sense, but they still put Lily to mind of a wedding vow and she jolted a little.

Mary took her hand again. "Then we should go back."

"Good," Lily said. "Good."

She wanted to take Alice's hand, but it was evident that the young women needed to be together. Strange that when she looked at her sister with George, she had seen the child Alice had always been. But standing next to Mary, she seemed more like the woman she was becoming.

George led the way and she walked beside him again, though unlike before she didn't touch him. She wanted to, wanted to feel that support from him again. And she did, just by his presence. Somehow she trusted him to fix this, even if there was no way her tangled mind could picture how that could be possible.

CHAPTER 17

Despite the drama of the afternoon, George's return with Lily, Alice and Mary wasn't met by much fanfare. For that he was grateful. His parents seemed to understand that what everyone needed was space, some time to gather themselves before they spoke again about the choices that now lay ahead.

Their friends had been called back from their searches and though he'd received several notes of relief that Alice had been found, the earls and their wives had also not pushed.

Now, after suppers that everyone had in their own quarters, he had come down to his father's study where they would talk about what would come next. And he would have to somehow find a way to keep his promise to Lily and Alice to fix this. To protect the sister of the woman he loved, and to perhaps even find a way to get to love Lily for the rest of his life.

The door behind him shut quietly and he turned to find only his father had joined him. The earl's face was lined with a deep frown, even as he crossed to the sideboard and poured them each a drink.

George smoothed his jacket. This room had very often been the place where he had received reprimands for poor behavior. He certainly deserved one now, even if his father didn't fully understand all he'd done.

"You must be deeply disappointed in me at present, my lord," he said softly.

His father arched a brow as he handed over the whisky he'd poured for him. "I was *disappointed* when you lost my prized stud horse at cards."

George stared at the amber liquid before him. There were some wild things he knew he'd never live down. "Eight years ago," he muttered softly.

His father surprised him by laughing, but it faded quickly enough. "Today I'm just...sorry, son. This feels like an unfair situation to everyone involved. But I don't understand how it got so out of control so quickly, nor why this entire arrangement was so rushed that we've come to this point."

George took a sip of his drink and thought of his mother. He thought of Lily and her suggestion that it wasn't right to keep the secret of her health from the family. It wasn't right for him to have to bear it all. In this moment, that felt very true. And yet he still wouldn't reveal her secret.

"Where is Lady Westinghouse?" he asked instead.

His father's mouth thinned with anger. "In her room. After her antics both today and from the beginning of all this, I don't think she needs to be in this meeting."

"Was she much trouble while we were all our searching?"

"She tried to be," the earl said and then gave a wicked little smile. "But Lady Delacourt put her firmly in her place. I don't think I've ever seen a woman so heavy with child who was also so patently terrifying. The viscountess was practically begging to be sequestered to her room by the end."

"Esme is a good friend to Lily," George said softly.

"She is that. I like her." His father cleared his throat. "Is Lady Westinghouse the one who bruised Mrs. Manning's face?"

The anger George had been trying to hold back all day rushed forward again as he recalled the blood on Lily's lip when she found him. Thought of the bruise that still marred her skin. He gripped his glass harder, until his knuckles went white.

"Yes," he said through clenched teeth. "She pushed Lily and caused her to fall and hit her head."

"*Lily,*" the earl said softly, but with meaning. "I like Lily even more than I like the countess."

George looked at his father once more. It was evident the old man had seen what he could no longer hide. And this secret *was* his. But did he trust the man who had betrayed his mother? Could the earl possibly understand what it was to love someone when he wasn't sure his father had such tender feelings for the wife he'd been lucky to have for over thirty years?

He didn't have to find an answer to that internal question, for the door to the study opened and his mother came in, followed by Lily and Alice, whose arms were linked. Lily almost seemed to be holding her sister up and Alice looked pale and small with continued fear and worry.

Lily immediately looked toward him and her gentle smile buoyed him up. Her support was like water and it flowed through him.

His mother closed the door behind them and gave a tired smile all around. "It's been a trying day, but I'm glad we could all meet here tonight. This isn't a topic that can wait another moment, I don't think."

"Very true, my dear," the earl agreed, and then went to the side-board. "May I get anyone else something to drink?"

The sisters demurred, as did George's mother. For a moment there was an awkward silence and then Alice, still gripping Lily's hand, stepped forward.

"I must apologize for all the dramatics caused by my behavior today," she said, her voice barely carrying even in the quiet room. "I've put you all in a terrible position."

"No," George replied. "A great many people put *you* in a dreadful position. But I think it's clear, just as I said earlier, that we cannot continue with this engagement."

His mother gripped the back of the closest chair and her eyes fluttered shut. He watched her carefully, ready to rush to her if this decision brought back the weakness that earlier worries had caused. But she opened her eyes again and met his. She nodded. "I think you're right, George. This was...poorly done in so many ways. I deeply apologize for my part in it."

The earl looked at his wife with what seemed like confusion. Of course, he knew not the impetus for all this. That the reasons for the engagement went beyond a normal arranged marriage and that was why it had been so rushed and fraught.

"I agree that this is for the best," Lily said. "But my stepmother has proven she'll be difficult if she loses what she created through her cruel blackmail."

Alice bent her head and the fear that moved through her was palpable even though she said nothing.

"And I promised you both earlier that I would fight to make sure she couldn't hurt you. I'll be like the god Ares. I will go to war to protect you if it comes to that."

Lily looked at him again, her breath coming in sharply at his use of the name that had first bonded them that night that felt like yesterday. That felt like decades ago at the same time, it had been so long since he'd been allowed to touch her.

His father stepped forward. "As my wife said, it's been a very long day. We've made this difficult decision and I think we all agree it's right. The engagement is broken and a night to think about how it would be best to handle it with the public would probably do us all good. I suggest we all get the rest that will clear our heads and meet again in the morning to discuss details."

"I think you're right, my lord," Lily said. "Thank you for your kindness in this troubling situation. You and the countess have been nothing but compassionate."

The earl inclined his head and then motioned for the door. Lily looked at George one last time and then she and her sister departed. When they were gone, his mother let out a great sigh. "I *am* tired."

"Then I'll escort you, Louisa," Lord Pembrooke said. "Good night, George. Don't ruminate over this too long, yes?"

George nodded even though he wasn't certain that was possible. He followed them up the stairs and down to his chamber. Once inside he stood at the bell, hand half extended to ring for his valet.

That would make the most sense, after all. To do as his family suggested and rest before the rest of decisions had to be made the next day. And yet there was one thought that continued to play in his mind over and over.

He was no longer engaged. He was free. The only obstacle that had kept him from touching Lily, kissing Lily, being near Lily, was gone now.

He found himself moving without truly meaning to, going to her. Hoping that when he knocked on her door she would answer and let him in, even if they hadn't fully resolved the future that had once kept them apart.

～

Lily had left Alice at her chamber, with a promise from her sister to lock her door and not let her mother in, even if she knocked. Alice had seemed happy to oblige and had gone inside where Lily assumed Mary was waiting. Lily found herself happy that her sister had someone to support and comfort her.

Now she sat in her own room, staring at the fire that glowed in the hearth. For the first time that day, it felt like she could *think*.

Despite how awful everything was and the scandal that was about to come, she felt lighter than she had in weeks. The reason was shameful, a proof of her selfishness that would make Prudence crow if she saw it.

George was free. He no longer belonged to her sister, there were no longer barriers that could separate them, at least not physically.

And all she wanted was to go to him, to feel his arms around her in comfort and passion. She wanted to relive that one beautiful night together and let herself forget her responsibilities even for just a little while.

She got to her feet, pivoted toward the door and threw it open to go to him, but as she did so, she found him standing there, hand raised as if he was about to knock.

Time slowed as they stared at each other, the realization that they both longed for the same thing becoming clear.

"Please let me in, Lily," he whispered, his voice low and rough, his eyes dark as stormy seas and filled with all the desire they'd been trying to repress.

There was no option to say no. She couldn't even recall that word existed. She caught his lapels and dragged him into the room. He pushed the door shut with his foot and pivoted, pressing her back against the barrier. Their mouths met with all the heat and desperation they'd been managing for weeks and it was like fireworks exploded in the wake.

Their tongues collided and she let out a needy moan that he answered with a deep one of his own. His hands gripped the fabric of her gown, bunching it around her lower back. She unbuttoned his jacket, shoving her hands inside the rough fabric to find the warmth of him beneath. When her palms moved over his chest through the layers of his waistcoat and shirt, they both moaned in time.

He pulled back and stared down into her face, his mouth turning down as he traced the line of the bruise on her cheek. She turned her lips into his palm and kissed him there.

"There's no pain," she whispered. "Not with you here."

He cupped her chin and tilted her face up and this time when he kissed her it was far more gentle and slow. She melted into him, reveling now in this kiss that she'd been dreaming of for weeks. How could she have lived without it? In this moment it felt as though it was required to survive.

His arms tightened around her and slowly he walked them both toward her bed. His fingers glided down her spine and she felt him flick the buttons of her gown open one by one.

"At Donville you didn't wear underthings," he whispered while he stroked up and down her spine against her chemise.

"At Donville I was Aphrodite," she said with a smile up at him.

"You'll always be Aphrodite to me," he said, and then he tugged her dress down.

It was odd, because he had seen her naked before. He had worshiped every inch of her body, but she'd worn a mask that night. They had been strangers. To have him stand before her in her underthings now, staring at her like she truly was a goddess felt... different.

After all they'd been through? All they knew about each other? It felt real.

"Are you blushing, Lily?" he asked, and the wicked tilt to his smile returned.

She reached up and tugged the chemise straps off her shoulders so she could push out of it. "Only in anticipation."

He didn't speak, but just stared at her now that she was naked save her stockings and slippers. His eyes were wide and he licked his lips like she was a feast and he a man starved.

"I wish I could wait," he said. "I wish I could do anything but claim like a barbarian, but it's been too long. And I feared I'd never get the chance to do this again."

She reached out and slipped a hand into the *v* of his waistcoat, then tugged him forward. "I want the claiming."

His mouth smashed to hers and the heat of desire lifted once more. There was nothing gentle to this, but she didn't want it to be gentle. She wanted to feel it, to know it was real, to be swept away by him and know that it wasn't the only time or the last time. She wanted to feel him and know he didn't belong to anyone else.

He lifted her to the edge of the bed and then stepped back. As she watched his every move, he untied his cravat, removed his waistcoat and tugged his shirt over his head.

"You really do look like a god," she said as she reached out to touch his chest. "Lucky Aphrodite."

He chuckled as he briefly stepped away to remove his boots and then returned, unfastening the fall front of his trousers as he did so. When they fell away she caught her breath.

This gorgeous, hard as steel, naked man was all hers to enjoy. She was shaking with anticipation as he moved to her, their faces even because of the high bed as he kissed her.

She opened her legs wider, giving him a place to step, and he took it, wedging his hips there as their naked bodies molded to each other.

"I want to look at you while I do this," he whispered, and reached between them to align their bodies. "Are you ready?"

She nodded. "I've been wanting this every moment of every day since the last time you touched me. I couldn't be more ready."

He pressed to her and she gasped as his cock slid inside the first inch. He watched her face as he took more and more, until he was fully seated in her already flexing body.

"You feel better than every fantasy," he moaned, kissing along the line of her jaw.

She arched against him and that broke the spell between them. He began to move, thrusting slowly at first, letting their bodies become accustomed to each other again. She met every stroke, grinding when their bodies fully merged. Already she felt the rising sensation of pleasure filling her, like she'd been on the edge all this time and now it was so, so easy to fall.

It seemed it was just as easy for him, for his face already twisted with the same pleasure that was rising in her. They ground together, their eyes locked, their bodies sliding against each other as if they'd been made to do so. The pleasure spiked, she reached for it, and then she was flying, her head falling back, her thighs gripping his hips, her sex clenching out of control.

"Fuck," he groaned as he dropped his head down against her shoulder and his mouth sucked along the line of her throat. God, the sensations that rippled through her, along every inch of her body. It was everything. He withdrew and the heat of him splashed between them.

She fell back against the bed and felt him move, his mouth gliding down her skin, over her breasts, down to her stomach. When he reached her thighs she sat up slightly, watching as he rubbed his stubbled cheek against the sensitive skin there.

His gaze flicked up to her, dark and wicked.

"What are you doing?" she asked, her voice catching.

"Tasting all that gorgeous pleasure," he said back as he brought his mouth to her.

She was already so sensitive from her orgasm that she jolted when he traced her clitoris with his tongue. He groaned like it meant as much to him and she fell back, lifting beneath him all over again as he sucked her, licked her, slid his fingers inside and pressed them to some magical place where the world turned rainbow colors.

When she came a second time, she pressed her hand to her lips, not wanting her moans and cries to bring the house down. He smiled as he licked her a few more times and then he came back up her body, tasting every inch of her before he slid her fully onto her bed and dragged her into his arms like she belonged there.

And for a little while, she let herself believe that she did.

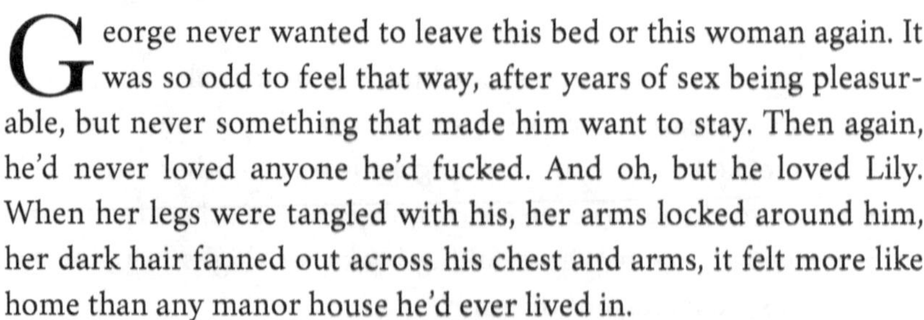

George never wanted to leave this bed or this woman again. It was so odd to feel that way, after years of sex being pleasurable, but never something that made him want to stay. Then again, he'd never loved anyone he'd fucked. And oh, but he loved Lily. When her legs were tangled with his, her arms locked around him, her dark hair fanned out across his chest and arms, it felt more like home than any manor house he'd ever lived in.

He kissed her forehead and smoothed his hand through her hair with a satisfied sigh. When she sighed, as well, it didn't sound quite as content.

"Where are those thoughts going, Lily?" he asked.

She cuddled a little closer, like she needed his warmth to answer the question. "I just don't know what's next. How can I protect my sister?"

He cupped her chin and tilted it up slightly. "Together."

"What are you saying?" she whispered.

"You *know* what I'm saying."

Her eyes widened as she leaned up on his chest a little. "If you not only end your engagement, but declare yourself for your former fiancée's sister, there will be no stopping the scandal. How would you ever recover?"

He could see her protective instincts still running overtime. Only this time she was turning them on him. The idea warmed him, that if he could manage to have a life with this woman, she would protect him for the rest of his days. He would do the same for her. They would do that together for their children and eventually their grandchildren if they were so blessed as to have them.

Only right now she couldn't see that future so clearly. And since everything else in both their lives had just gone off like an explosion, he was willing to give it time. As long as he could still be near her, the rest would come.

"Hmmm, I think I can recover much faster if you kiss me," he teased as he set her hand gently on his already half-hard cock.

She laughed and it was like music. When he slid her beneath him and the laughter turned to a shaky sigh, that was even better.

"Now let's try all that again," he murmured as he kissed the angle of her jaw. "But this time much, much slower."

CHAPTER 18

It had only been a few hours since Lockhart left her bed with sweet kisses and even sweeter promises that he'd be back. The pleasure of their night together had lingered for a long time, but as morning light dawned and the reality of what was to come grew larger, Lily's calm had faded. There was nothing resolved when it came to the future for her sister or for Lockhart. Those things would have to be determined before anything else could even be discussed.

She drew in a deep breath and knocked on her sister's door.

"It's Lily," she said, so her sister wouldn't worry that it was Prudence. Her stepmother had not been seen nor heard from since she'd been relegated to her rooms the day before, but Lily had no doubt that could and would eventually change.

The lock clicked and Alice opened the door. She looked tired, but much more at peace than she had in the weeks before. There was no denying that the end of the engagement was good for her and Lily smiled as she embraced her gently.

"Good morning," Alice said. "Will you sit with us?"

Us. Lily looked past her to find Mary sitting at the table across the room. When their eyes met, Mary shifted with discomfort.

"Thank you, that would be nice."

Lily followed her sister to the table. Alice took her seat and immediately took Mary's hand. When Mary looked at her it was with deep affection, just as it had always been. Before Lily had taken it for friendship after they'd been raised so closely, but now she saw it for what it was. This love wasn't new. It had probably been brewing for years and years.

"We'll have our final discussions with Lord Lockhart and Lord and Lady Pembrooke this morning," Lily said.

Color flooded Alice's cheeks. "Yes. And Mama. I'm sure she won't keep herself from those conversations. I'm shocked the earl and countess could keep her clear until now."

"You have a great many allies on your side," Lily said. "The Pembrookes, all the other earls and countesses in attendance. They might not know the entire truth of what has happened, no one would force that from you."

"Except for my mother," Alice said with a tinge of bitterness. "I assume *she* is the one who told Lockhart."

Lily pursed her lips. "Yes. She did. And I admit, I don't know if she revealed the truth to anyone else in her upset. But no one has said anything to me. You don't have to cut yourselves open. But as for me, as for George—Lord Lockhart, we are determined to protect you and stand with you in whatever the future looks like. You aren't alone in this, neither of you."

She looked to Mary and at last the young woman lifted her gaze. Her eyes were filled with wonder. "You've always been so kind, Mrs. Manning. If you would extend even a little bit of that to me, I would be grateful."

"*Lily*," Lily said, reaching across to take Mary's free hand. "If you and my sister are in love, if you mean so much to her, then I really think you must call me Lily."

Bright tears filled Mary's eyes and she exchanged a meaningful look with Alice before she got up. "I'll leave you two alone for a moment."

Alice smiled at her as she left for the adjoining dressing room. "She's afraid."

"Yes, I know. Prudence has a great deal of control over her, over you. But I swear to you that I won't let that stand."

Her sister tilted her head. "Yes. I believe you. When you speak about a future, it's impossible *not* to believe it. I have hope that this will work out, despite all the fraught beginnings and upset."

Funny, that was exactly how Lily felt when she thought about George. Though working it out for them might be very different. She could be, and she had no doubt would be, his lover. The rest would have to be discussed because she wouldn't ruin him. "Well, you aren't unprotected."

Alice looked at her evenly. "I suppose you've always done that, to your detriment even. Are you…are you in love with Lockhart?"

Lily's lips parted. "I—why would you ask me that?"

"I saw the way you looked at each other when you found me and Mary in the woods. The way you kept turning to him for support. The way I never did to him or he to me. I was so tangled up in my own fears I couldn't see it before yesterday afternoon."

With a shaky breath, Lily considered her answer. It was one thing to not love the man and not want to marry him, it was another to find out your own sister had been with him. She feared Alice might view her differently, but if anything had been learned in the last few weeks, it was that honesty was the way forward.

"We—we met before I came here." She worried her hands on the table. "Neither of us realized who the other was that night, as we had never met before. And there was a connection right away, I can't deny it."

"Even though you tried," Alice said softly.

"Because I didn't want to hurt you."

"But what about you?" Alice asked with a shake of her head that made golden curls bob around her face. "You lost love once, so to find it again—"

Lily took her hand. "I-I didn't love Thomas. It wasn't a happy marriage."

Alice's mouth dropped open. "You didn't? Why didn't you tell me? Oh...to protect me."

"Yes. I didn't want you to know that I'd been pushed into the marriage by your mother. That it was miserable." She sighed.

Alice took both her hands. "You raised me. We never talk about it, but we both know it's true. Perhaps you see me as just a little girl, but I'm not."

"No. You're most definitely not," Lily admitted.

"I want us to be sisters, as we always should have been. I want us to be honest, to be able to hurt in front of each other."

Lily nodded. "That's fair. I do love him, Alice. I have no idea if that will be something that can be fully pursued, there are so many issues."

"Perhaps the only issue that matters is love."

Lily smiled at the idea. There was such hope in that even if she couldn't quite believe it yet. "You sound very wise."

"I told you, I'm all grown up," Alice said with a little laugh.

There was a light knock on the door and they heard Reeves' voice outside. "The family is ready for you, Mrs. Manning, Miss Westinghouse."

Their eyes met and Lily grasped her sister's hand. "Let's go face this together."

~

George turned from the fire as Lily and Alice entered his father's study arm in arm. His breath caught at the sight of Lily, so beautiful despite no sleep the night before. She smiled softly at him and his world was right, no matter what happened next.

And Alice also looked entirely changed. For weeks, months, she had seemed pinched, uncertain, sad. Now her expression was open, her eyes were bright. There was fear there, of course, but she looked happy.

"Good morning," his father said, and motioned for the two women to sit. Once they had in two chairs, the earl and the countess took their place on the settee and George stood before the fire between them.

Lord Pembrooke cleared his throat and looked first at his son and then at his wife. "I haven't been able to stop thinking about how we got here," he began. "And I'm realizing that there is more to this than just an advantageous match for both parties. So I'm asking you, either of you, *any* of you, why did this happen?"

George tensed and glanced at Lily, who was now leaning forward on her chair. Then he looked at his mother. She was pale and gripped the edge of the settee with one hand.

"Tell him," he said softly.

She glanced at her husband and then nodded. "A few months ago, I was told that I have an illness. Dr. Browning was sparing with the details, but he was clear about one thing: there is no fixing it. There is no way to know how much time there is left, but it will end my life and sooner rather than later. Because of that, I asked George to stop his wild ways and marry, so that I might see him settled before my life ended."

The earl sat stock still as his wife explained, his shoulders stiff and his expression unreadable. "Dying," he finally said softly.

Lady Pembrooke's eyes filled with tears and then she nodded. "Yes."

George might have guessed at many ways his father would react to such news, but he never would have said the earl would drop to his knees before the settee, grasp his wife's hands and stare at her while silent tears started down his face.

Lily got up then. She went to George and took his hand. He realized he, too, had tears on his cheeks and when she touched him the weight of the pain lifted just a fraction.

"This cannot be," his father choked out. "No, Louisa. Not this."

"I'm afraid so," she whispered, and the terror she hadn't ever fully shown George was clear on her face.

"Why didn't you tell me?" the earl asked. When his wife was silent, he bent his head, shame on every line of his countenance. George had never seen that before. That grief of regret. "B-because of what I did to you over the years. Because you feared I wouldn't care the way you needed me to."

Alice very kindly got up and went to the window, staring out and giving the family some space. Lily didn't move. She only held George's hand tighter.

"I'm here," she whispered.

He nodded to her, holding her gentle stare a moment to ease the spinning around him.

"I love you, Louisa. I have been piss poor at showing it, but you are my world," his father confessed, with a great deal more passion than George had ever heard him talk about anything. "My God, I think of the years I wasted being a fool, acting as a man of my station instead of the man you deserved."

George drew back at that statement. Not only because it showed him that his father might not have always loved his mother well, but he had loved her truly. He also couldn't help but be struck by that notion of wasted years.

Would that be what George lamented if he waited for the time to be "right" or for there be a time when no scandal would touch what he felt for Lily? Would he hate himself for not being more courageous or stronger? Would he lose her because he wasn't brave enough, hadn't been brave enough since the first moment he touched her and realized in some deep, primal place that she was his?

"I forgive you," Louisa said. "I forgave you long ago, the moment you came back to me and I could see that you had changed. If my life is to be shorter than I hoped, I also want the last weeks or months or years of it to be good and happy. And with you."

"They will be," Lord Pembrooke promised, and kissed both her hands. "They will be. For all of us."

He looked back at George and he knew his parents would also support whatever he did. Hadn't they always, even when they shook their heads or rolled their eyes at his antics? Neither of them would hesitate if he declared a future that was as bright as he wanted it to be. And if they did? Well, it didn't matter.

Because he was going to claim it.

He turned toward Lily. "I love you. I love you, Lily."

Her lips parted and she glanced at his parents with a blush.

"I know, I know this isn't the optimal way to do this, but wasted time is the worst waste of all. My father has just reminded me of that. I almost lost you because both of us were trying to live for the happiness of others. I cannot do that again. Lily, I want to marry you."

~

"George," Lily somehow managed to choke out when she couldn't breathe and all she could see was him, even though his parents were both staring at them and Alice had jolted back toward them with a little gasp.

He never looked away from her. And there was no denying that every word he said, he meant. "I *love* you," he repeated. "Enough to face whatever comes, as long as it's us together."

Lily struggled to respond, not because she wasn't certain of her feelings or his. She was very clear on both. But she had lived a life trying to please others. It was a hard habit to break.

"I was married a-a long time," she said softly. "And didn't have children. Your legacy is tied to that ability. If I denied you that…" She trailed off, for she couldn't further voice that personal pain.

George stared at her. "You never mentioned this before."

She shook her head. "You never could have been mine before. What would have been the point?"

Lord Pembrooke cleared his throat and without releasing his wife's hand stepped a little closer. "It isn't my place to interrupt, but if you did not have children with Thomas Manning, it was more likely his fault rather than anything to do with you."

George's eyes went wide even as Lily's cheeks burned at this uncouth subject. "What do you mean?"

"Er, this will be indelicate but when we were youths we all used to make these idiotic wagers. Manning was the worst of them. One memorable one was when he claimed he could walk the length of a fence rail surrounding one of the meanest bulls in the county. He tried, the bull bumped the fence and Manning fell straight down with the fence…er…well he landed quite hard on his…"

George's brows lifted. "He smashed his bollocks?"

"George!" his mother gasped out and Alice lifted her hands to bright red cheeks.

Lily couldn't be shocked though. Not by the crude description at any rate. Her surprise came from the crux of the story, itself. "But he…he blamed me for my lack of breeding," she whispered.

"Oh Lily," Alice breathed with tears in her eyes.

"To do so was a cruelty to be certain," Pembrooke said with a kind expression. "But likely untrue."

"And even if it weren't," Lady Pembrooke said. "Do you think I would separate my son from a woman who makes him look at her like that?"

Lily glanced at him and found George was staring at her and there was nothing but love on his face. Powerful, pure, unshakeable love that was nothing like she'd ever dreamed of for herself.

"Yes, just like that," Lady Pembrooke said with a sigh. "There's *always* a chance that a marriage won't produce children. If this one doesn't, my husband has brothers and they have sons and there will be someone to carry on this name in the end. I wouldn't take George away from you for some unknown grandchildren who may or may not ever exist no matter who he weds."

There was some relief to that but Lily still met George's stare. "The only opinion on the topic that matters is yours."

"I want you," he said. "I've made that clear enough, haven't I? I don't care about anything else."

"Yes, you do," Lily said with a shake of her head. "The last months have proven that. And there *will* be a scandal. It's unavoidable. What if we hurt—"

"My dear," his mother said. "It isn't my place to interrupt this proposal even if I keep doing so, but if you fear hurting me or my husband, we have endured a great many scandals thanks to this rogue. This one would be a *pleasure* to navigate because it will obviously bring him happiness."

"Thank you, Mama," he said.

His father put his arm around Lady Pembrooke's waist. "And it might also solve your other problem. If you two are married, that would allow Alice to live with you. After all, you would certainly have the ability to provide her with a great deal."

Lily looked toward her. "That's true," she whispered. "*Alice* could live with us. And you would never be in danger from…from anyone ever again."

Alice caught her breath because it was clear the facts that had been unspoken. Mary would live with them, as well. Mary would be safe. And ultimately, they would be free to be together, at least in Lily and George's walls.

"I would be certain of it," George said. "For you, Alice. But also for Lily."

Alice stepped up and touched his hand. "I did not want to call you husband, but I would be very happy to call you brother. Lily, this man and his family are working hard to resolve all your fears. You mustn't refuse him. Please, do this for yourself. Embrace the happiness and love you've always deserved."

His father let out a chuckle. "And now, my boy, you seem to have the unsolicited advice and blessing of a roomful of onlookers. We'll leave you now to finish convincing my lovely future daughter-in-law to say yes."

Lily blinked at his certainty and smiled as he patted her hand before he guided his wife and her sister from the room and left her alone with George.

"We never do things in the right order, have you noticed that?" he said, his face bright and filled with mischievous pleasure she hadn't seen there before.

She felt the same on her own face, despite her misgivings. "Are you truly certain?" she asked. "Their interruptions and blessings aside, certain for *yourself*."

"Perhaps I'm not being clear. Lily, I don't want to be like my father, riddled with regrets for what I didn't do for the woman I love. There could never be regrets about knowing I did everything for her. And you are her. I love you. I'll repeat it a thousand times if it helps. And I'll repeat my question as often as I need to: Will you marry me?"

There was a sweet anxiousness to his expression now. As if he didn't know her heart. But then again, she hadn't said it to him yet because of the barriers that had stood between them, both real and imagined.

She touched his face. "I love you, too, George. So deeply, so powerfully, so truly. To be your wife would be a dream."

"Is that a yes, then?" he pressed.

She pressed her forehead to his, feeling their breath mingle and suddenly all her fears felt so much lighter. "Yes," she said. And then she shouted it. "Yes! Yes! Yes!"

He only silenced her with a kiss and she was very happy to end the conversation in such a way. Or start it. Or continue it. As long as he was hers.

〜

"She'll never allow this," Alice said as she walked through the hallway with Lily and George.

Lily looked up at George and he felt strong as a quarter horse when she did. "I'm not asking her," he said. "I'm telling her."

They opened the door to the parlor where Lady Westinghouse awaited them. He felt the shift in both women. The fear he wanted to erase from both their lives. And he would in time.

"Good morning, Lady Westinghouse," he said. "Thank you for waiting for us. I'm sure you have a great many questions."

"I do," she snapped, and glared at her daughter and stepdaughter. "Where did you run to, you ungrateful thing? How did Lily convince you to ruin all this?"

Alice clutched Lily's hand. "Lily didn't do *anything*, Mama. And you know why I ran. You were happy to shout it to my former fiancé without any thought for me."

"It's unnatural," the viscountess said. "And you shall not do such a thing in my house."

"You are correct, she will not," George said. "Because she won't live in your house. Not ever again."

Lady Westinghouse's eyes went wide. "Does that mean the wedding is still on? Gracious, why didn't you say so? This is all forgotten. Of course you would do the right thing—"

It was troubling how quickly the woman could go from rage to sickly sweet. George raised a hand to interrupt her. "There will be a wedding, but not between Alice and me. I will marry Lily. And Alice will come to live with us, under our care."

All the color left Lady Westinghouse's face and she pivoted toward Lily. "You little bitch!" she screeched. "How could you?"

She stepped toward Lily, and George put out a hand to stop her. "Have a care, my lady," he said. "In how you speak to and act toward my future wife. There are many ways this can end for you and some of them will allow you to have some of the same benefits you wanted when it was Alice you blackmailed into this marriage."

She jerked her gaze toward him. "What are you saying?"

"You could still have a connection to the house of Pembrooke if you can manage to control yourself." He hated to offer that to her, but if it freed Lily and Alice from her cruelty, he would do so.

There was a long pause and he couldn't read the viscountess's expression as she glared at Lily and Alice, then back at him.

"And what about a settlement for the broken engagement?" she asked at last. "If Alice goes to live with you, I somehow doubt I shall be able to arrange another."

"I will not marry, Mama," Alice said.

George looked at her with pride. She was afraid and yet she still spoke up for herself. There was a flash of Lily's strength in her, it seemed. And he admired her for it. "You heard her. Yes, I'm sure we can arrange a settlement. An annuity, I think would be best, the payment of which determined by your behavior."

"What would be the terms?" Lady Westinghouse asked through what seemed like clenched teeth.

"Easy enough, or at least they should be. You will not speak against Alice or Lily. Ever. And you will not bother either of them. If you're lucky enough that either of them wishes to see you, you'll allow that to be their choice. Step out of line and the payments stop."

Lady Westinghouse glanced toward them. It was clear she was angry, but she was also greedy and grasping. The second seemed to eclipse the first. "Fine," she hissed out.

He moved closer to her. "And if you ever put a hand on Lily again, I will make you sorrier than you can imagine. I will destroy your world with a flick of my wrist and I'll never think twice about it."

Her eyes widened at the statement and the quiet rage behind it. She nodded and then glanced at Lily. "I am sorry, my dear. You know I didn't mean for you to fall."

Lily straightened her spine. "I'm certain you didn't. Now perhaps it would make the most sense for you to go back to London as soon as possible."

She nodded. "Yes. I'll look for the full terms and a first payment from my solicitors there."

She hustled from the room and Alice sighed. "She didn't even say goodbye."

George moved to her and took her hands. "I am sorry, Alice. But I'm so very happy that you'll have a place with your sister and I. And that we'll get a chance to know your Mary and see your life unfold in the way you wish."

"Lily is right," Alice said with a little smile. "You truly are a good man. And now I leave you to this very good man, Lily. I'll be sure the friends and family are all gathered for the celebration."

She kissed Lily's cheek and squeezed George's hand before she slipped from the room.

"Will she be well?" he asked.

Lily looked up at him. "She will. Thanks to you."

"Thanks to *you*," he said in return. Then he touched her face, the face he would see beside him all of his days. "I wonder how much time we have before we'll be expected to join the others?"

She laughed. "Not enough, you wicked thing."

He drew her closer in his arms and lowered his mouth to hers. "You underestimate my abilities, my love."

EPILOGUE

F*ive Years Later*

Lady Pembrooke's life extended far more than months. She lived to see Lily and George marry. To see them welcome their son and their daughter within three years of that very happy union. She celebrated birthdays and anniversaries and the blooming of her garden with her husband at her side. And George had never seen him so devoted and happy to be with her.

When she finally left them, peacefully and quietly one day as she lay with the sunlight streaming in over her bed, it was with her family surrounding her.

And now they gathered, a year later, with all their friends and family to celebrate her life again, and to laugh and love together despite their sadness.

George stood back from it all, watching this magnificent group of people. His father sat with his grandson on his lap. At four, there was no one little Edward adored more than the old man. He thought his son might actually be his father's best friend and he loved the relationship between them.

His daughter, Louisa after her beloved grandmother, was with Esme and Delacourt's little girl, given her mother's birth name

Charlotte. Though Esme always said she named her daughter after a girl she used to know. The two children were spinning in the middle of the room, their hair streaming out and riotous giggles rising above the din of the adults talking. Every once in a while, Marianne and Ramsbury's son, Patrick, poked his head from behind his mother's skirts and stuck his tongue out at them.

In another corner of the room Campbell Ripley, the famous boxing instructor and good friend of all the earls, stood with his son, Ian, holding up his hands for the little boy to thwack with great, laughing gusto and unsurprisingly natural talent.

Clarissa stood with the Ramsbury's and Jane, Ripley's wife. His cousin's newborn son Benedict was in her arms and the two women were cooing over him. There was such joy to his favorite cousin now. Such an ease that had never existed before she met Kirkwood.

And by the window were Alice and Mary, alongside Jane's sister Nora and her husband, Eldon Granger. Over the years the two women had become comfortable in showing the true heart of their relationship with their little group of friends. They'd been fully accepted and protected by the group, and by his parents when Alice had felt ready to reveal the truth to them several years earlier. Mary had become a fixture at their home, then, as well. Welcomed as a partner to a member of the family just as all the other husbands and wives had been.

It had often been said to him, when they were engaged, that Alice would grow into herself with time. With love, she had done just that and he deeply admired his sister-in-law and Mary for what they had overcome and all they had made for themselves.

Had there been scandal with the end of their engagement and his hasty marriage to Lily? Indeed. In some corners, they were still not accepted. But somehow it hadn't stung quite as much as anyone had feared it might. In fact, it had the wonderful effect of letting George know exactly who his real friends were.

He smiled as the best of them, Kirkwood, approached, a drink in hand. "This is a madhouse."

"I know," George said, and they clinked their glasses together. "And it's all ours. Isn't it divine?"

They smiled together and watched over the group for a moment. Then Roderick turned toward him. "I've always wanted to ask you a question."

"Oh, that's terrifying. Ask away," George said with a laugh.

"When did you know you were in love with Lily?" he asked.

Lily was entering the room as the question was asked, her dress laying against the swell of her belly, which currently contained their third child. She was glowing with happiness as she slipped up next to Esme and wrapped an arm around her old friend.

God, but she was beautiful. He was always stricken by that fact whenever he saw her.

"From the first moment," he said without hesitation. "Before I knew her face, before I knew her name, I loved her."

Roderick smiled. "It's funny, isn't it? You denied the existence of lightning and I thought I required it. And here we got the reverse."

"It's not funny," George said. "It's perfect."

"That it is, old friend." Roderick ducked to grab one of the little girls as they raced past and she squealed with delight as he carried her off to her own father.

That left George to cross the room to his wife. She stepped away from their friends and children and into his arms. He kissed her, not caring that everyone could see, and rested a hand on her stomach.

"Good afternoon, Aphrodite. What can I go to war over for you today?"

She laughed at his teasing. "I think what I want most is a little tea and one of those cakes. And you."

"Well, I will go to war for the first, but as for me?" He kissed her again. "I am and ever shall be *yours*."

EXCERPT OF ONCE UPON A COURTESAN

THE COMERFORD COURTESANS BOOK 1
(OCTOBER 7, 2025)

**Coming Soon from Jess Michaels
A New Series about Three Infamous Sisters**

Arabella looked in the direction that she indicated and her smile widened as her old friend and mentor started across the room toward them. She was wearing a gorgeous dark blue silk that brought out the absolute perfection of her skin. Arabella could only hope she would age so well and still be so sought after at the long end of her thirties.

"Simone," she said and hugged her friend. Her sisters did the same and then stepped away a little. They were all close to Simone, but her sisters knew that Arabella and Simone were the closest. "My God, you are a vision. I'm desperately jealous."

Simone barked out a burst of laughter and linked arms with her. For a moment they looked out over the group of courtesans.

"We might need to offer a little assistance to Beatrice Holms," Simone said. "She's not had much luck with her choice of protectors and her last didn't settle her well."

"Oh, poor Bea, she's so new," Arabella said with a sigh. "Yes, I'll be on the lookout for her."

"What about yourself?" Simone asked, repeating the question Arabella's sisters had just posted, but with far more experience behind the words. "Who will you pick, do you think?"

"Oh, it's early days yet," Arabella said with a knowing smile. "I'm not allowing anyone near."

Unlike her sisters, who had seemed troubled by the answer, Simone nodded knowingly. "Ah, so you let them work themselves into a froth for you. Fight over the honor of your attention. You increase your value."

"I learned from the best," Arabella said.

"Hmmm," Simone replied. "That's a lovely compliment, but I think you've surpassed me in your reputation and accomplishments in these last five years. You are the ultimate courtesan and one we all strive to emulate."

"You shall make me blush," Arabella said with a shake of her head. "I didn't think I still knew how to do that."

Simone laughed and then squeezed Arabella's arm gently. "I do have some information for you that might just change your thought process on your next lover."

Arabella's eyebrows lifted. "Really? And what is that?"

"Silas is back."

It felt as though the room around Arabella faded into a blur, the music stopping, the buzz of the women dissipating into the wind. There was nothing but her and Simone then, and the name that hung between them.

"Silas Windham," she managed to choke out.

Simone nodded. "The very one."

Simone was watching her closely now. But of course she would. Silas and that night at the Vauxhall Gardens had brought Arabella to her and to this life. She'd never made her desire for him a secret over the years because she had decided never to make what she wanted a secret ever again. She pursued her passions, whether it be men, the occasional woman, orgasms or the finest silk for a gown.

"Back from America," Arabella mused.

"Yes, I saw him at the Donville Masquerade two nights ago."

"Oh," Arabella said slowly. "Does that mean he's yours?"

"Mine?" Simone cackled. "My dear he was never mine. That moment in the garden altered your life, I know, but it was, as I've told you many times over the years, nothing but a bit of fun for me. Silas has never *belonged* to anyone, I don't think."

There was far too much pleasure in the idea that the man was fair game. Arabella had to fight for breath as she murmured, "Hmmmm."

"So he's yours to claim if you'd like him."

She tossed a lock of hair off her shoulder with a shrug that was far more nonchalant than she actually felt. "We shall see. Who even knows what kind of man he'd be after his long disappearance. What brought him back anyway?"

A little shadow crossed Simone's expression, but then she shrugged. "I have my theories, but he didn't say. Silas has always blown by his own wind. Rather like someone else I know."

"Sounds like it could be explosive," Arabella said.

"I fear it might be. But I may see him at Vivien's party tomorrow. Are you going?"

"No. My aunt is having us over for our monthly supper at her home."

"Oh, sweetest Caroline. Give her my regards," Simone said.

Arabella laughed for her proper aunt had only encountered Simone once but any mention of the courtesan always made her blush.

"And should I make an overture to Silas on your behalf?" Simone continued. "Set the groundwork for you?"

A shiver worked through Arabella at that thought and yet she still shrugged as if it didn't matter. "I suppose."

"Then I shall. And now I must go. Harding is expecting me soon and one mustn't disappoint."

"Goodbye dearest," Arabella said, kissing her cheek. Her sister floating toward Simone, as well, saying their goodbyes, too.

But as Arabella stood there, still watching the room but no longer seeing it, she couldn't deny the thrill that worked through her body and soul. The man she had dreamed of, obsessed over, fantasized about as back. And she was going to make him hers.

There was already no doubt about it.

Pre-Order Once Upon a Courtesan at retailers everywhere now! Available for download on October 7, 2025!

ALSO BY JESS MICHAELS

The Comerford Courtesans

Once Upon a Courtesan (October 7, 2025)

When the Earl Was Wicked (January 6, 2026)

The Trouble With Seduction (April 7, 2026)

About An Earl

The Wallflower List

The Hellion's Secret

The Accidental Countess

The Courtesan's Protector

The Lady Once Known As

Theirs

Their Marchioness

Their Duchess

Their Countess

Their Bride

Their Viscountess

The Kent's Row Duchesses

No Dukes Allowed

Not Another Duke

Not the Duke You Marry

The 1797 Club

The Daring Duke

Her Favorite Duke

The Broken Duke

The Silent Duke

The Duke of Nothing

The Undercover Duke

The Duke of Hearts

The Duke Who Lied

The Duke of Desire

The Last Duke

To see a complete listing of Jess Michaels' titles, please visit:

http://www.authorjessmichaels.com/books

ABOUT THE AUTHOR

USA Today Bestselling author Jess Michaels likes geeky stuff, Vanilla Coke Zero, anything coconut, cheese and her dog, Elton. She is lucky enough to be married to her favorite person in the world and lives in Oregon settled between the ocean and the mountains.

When she's not out birding or rewatching Bob's Burgers over and over and over (she's a Tina), she writes historical romances with smoking hot characters and emotional stories. She has written for numerous publishers and is now fully indie.

Jess loves to hear from fans! So please feel free to contact her at Jess@AuthorJessMichaels.com.

Jess Michaels offers a free book to members of her newsletter, so sign up on her website:
http://www.AuthorJessMichaels.com/

facebook.com/JessMichaelsBks

instagram.com/JessMichaelsBks

bookbub.com/authors/jess-michaels

9 781958 358351